CIRCLE OF
SHAMAN

CIRCLE OF
SHAMAN

Healing Through Ecstasy, Rhythm, and Myth

KAREN BERGGREN

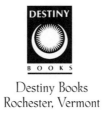

Destiny Books
Rochester, Vermont

Destiny Books
One Park Street
Rochester, Vermont 05767
www.gotoit.com

Library of Congress Cataloging-in-Publication Data
Berggren, Karen A., 1953–
    Circle of shaman : healing through ecstasy, rhythm, and myth /
    Karen A. Berggren.
        p.   cm.
    Includes bibliographical references.
    ISBN 0-89281-622-8 (pbk. : alk. paper)
    1. Shamanism—Miscellanea. I. Title.
BF1611.B46   1998   97-44362
291.1'44—dc21   CIP

Printed and bound in the United States

10 9 8 7 6 5 4 3 2 1

Text design and layout by Kristin Camp
This book was typeset in Garamond with Phaistos as the display type.

Destiny Books is a division of Inner Traditions International

Distributed to the book trade in Canada by Publishers Group West (PGW), Toronto, Ontario
Distributed to the book trade in the United Kingdom by Deep Books, London
Distributed to the book trade in Australia by Millennium Books, Newtown, N.S.W.
Distributed to the book trade in New Zealand by Tandem Press, Auckland
Distributed to the book trade in South Africa by Alternative Books, Ferndale

To Rya, with all my love, respect, and admiration. Without you, I would be telling a different story.
And to the One Heart, pulsing ecstatically throughout the web connecting All.

Never doubt that a small group of thoughtful, committed people can change the world. Indeed, it is the only thing that ever can.
Margaret Mead

These are the times. We are the people.
Jean Houston

We must assume our existence as broadly as we in any way can;
Everything, even the unheard of, must be possible in it.
This is at bottom the only courage that is demanded of us:
To have courage for the most strange, the most inexplicable.
Rainer Maria Rilke

Contents

Foreword

Karen Berggren's *Circle of Shaman* is a wonderful gift that will be adored by everyone interested in shamanic experience. This is her personal story of entering the shaman's world and how her journey takes us into the heart of ecstatic experience.

Today's growing interest in shamanism has led to an acknowledgment of the power of imaginal realms, the space where archetypal presences grace us in visionary encounter. In our drumming and calling forth of totemic relations, we have been reshown old ways of healing.

Yet, in spite of this contemporary revival of the shamanic way, something of vital importance has been left out and kept in the dark. We have forgotten that the heart of shamanism is nothing less than unfettered ecstatic experience and this is what Karen Berggren awakens us to remember. The word shaman originally referred to the excited, often shaking, body of a person filled with life's spirit. As an old Micmac medicine man once told me, "No shake, no shaman."

To enter the heart of shamanism is to enter the core of ecstatic experience. Karen Berggren fully understands this and her exciting text, which weaves inspiring prose, narrative, and academic research, brings a much needed healing to the over-sober scene in contemporary shamanism.

I know firsthand that she is in the center of shamanic work and have experienced her move to the rhythms of the dancing drum. Open your eyes and ears and heart to what she has to say. Her work promises to open your heart and carry you into the ecstasy of life, the truest place of myth where we find ourselves at home in the Circle of Shaman.

Bradford Keeney, Ph.D., author of Shaking Out the Spirits.

Preface

The following story is taken from a period in my life spanning seven years, from 1989 to 1996. I tell it through recollection, journal entries, and confirmation of details with those who've journeyed with me in physical bodies and without. It is a true story of my unexpected and initially dubious meeting with a group in spirit, the Circle of Shaman, and their subsequent teachings on the healing power of rhythm and the ecstatic experience.

The teachings act not so much as an introduction to a new body of knowledge, but more like memory triggers into the dynamics and understandings of a larger field of consciousness in which we all participate. This larger field has been called by many names: the sacred realm, the mythic realm, the collective unconscious, the transpersonal, God, Goddess, the Great Mystery, the Dreamtime, the One Heart, the Tao, and others. This expanded consciousness permeates the substrata of our beings, existing primarily below the horizon of conscious awareness. Many spiritual traditions hold that our physical world is an emanation of this greater sacred realm; thus there is an intimate link between the two. The reality of this link and the deeper world hints at itself through myth, dreams, premonitions, intuition, miracles, visionary encounters, and ecstatic experiences.

Ecstasy reveals this link that bridges the worlds of the sacred and mundane, allowing psychological travel between the two. But what's the significance of taking such a journey? Shamans first framed the answer more than thirty thousand years ago. The basis for their vocation is the belief that when you travel into the sacred realm and address or resolve issues there, your efforts will have a corresponding effect in physical reality.

In shamanic terms, the flight of ecstasy is the experience of union and communion with the sacred realm.

Throughout time, techniques for invoking ecstasy have been cultivated and revered for healing self and community, gaining knowledge, dialoguing with spirits and mythic beings, and living in greater harmony with the earth. Many of these techniques involve drumming, dancing, and chanting, all of which seek to entrain the participant to the rhythms of this deeper reality and open the doorway to the ecstatic experience.

Whether arrived at intentionally or unplanned, ecstasy often soaks your awareness with a sense of familiarity, vitality, community, and synergy that allows you to tap deep wellsprings of healing, creativity, and compassion. It opens the heart and mind to insights, hidden potentials, and vital possibilities for transformation.

Why is such an endeavor important today? Researchers are exploring evidence that suggests consciousness evolves through contact with the sacred or mythic realm, experiences that the psyche renders in the form of images and stories. The insights or revelations gained from ecstatic experiences—the basis of these stories—help foster personal healing and societal innovations that evolve the psyche into greater levels of complexity over time. As shamans have traditionally been healers and myth-keepers charged with the survival and well-being of their tribe, it is no exaggeration to say that today that task has fallen into the laps of us all. As old paradigms continue to crumble around us, our well-being and survival will ultimately be determined by the ability to transform our guiding stories, to work in partnership with the earth, spirit, and each other, and to learn how to think in entirely new ways. Ecstasy, as a sacred technology, is unparalleled in its contribution to these efforts.

At times when my feelings of gratitude and appreciation for the Circle of Shaman have tilted too far into veneration, they've counseled me not to worship or romanticize them in any way.

The Circle of Shaman's primary purpose is to collaborate with us in the Great Awakening, an evolutionary leap of consciousness taking place at this time upon the earth. Their role is to encourage and support our journey by illuminating ecstatic pathways into the sacred realm where a greater presence awaits to spark our memories of the magical nature of consciousness and to nourish the seeds of our becoming.

Acknowledgments

I wish to gratefully acknowledge those friends, teachers, and loved ones who have played a significant role in this journey: Reverend Stephen Fulton and Reverend Simeon Stefanidakis at the First Spiritual Temple in Brookline, Massachusetts, for their excellent teachings in mediumship; the Arcana Drummers and cyberspace community who shared the tentative early steps; Carole Fretts, who took the inner plunge with me long ago; Larry Daloz, who gave me courage to enter the dark; David Kantor who critically, but kindly, observed that I was better at writing than at office management; Linda Samay and my corporate colleagues for supporting a flexible work schedule allowing me to write; John Perkins for asking, "So when do you plan to write a book?" and directing me to Inner Traditions; Bradford Keeney, technician of the sacred, for his ecstatic spirit and for breathing his soul into my work; Sanderson Beck for helpful editorial suggestions; my kindred spirits in Sister Adsum, Rhythm Alive!, Circle, Skin, and Bone, Drumbodhi, and Tantric Rhythm Riders, where we've shared the Good News on drums and the stories of Black Hawk with the people; Imani Buchanan, Dean Buchanan, and Mo Ching Yip for sharing their love and knowledge of the drum and dance; Donald Koch, for his support and creation of the sacred writing space where this book was birthed; Blake Himm, for his passion for drumming, ritual, and bending the time; Jimi and Morwen Two Feathers, cofounders of Earth Drum Council, and the drum and dance community they have infused with vitality and devotion; Morwen, adept spiritual midwife and godmother to the work, whose love, wisdom, and editing prowess ensured this birth was a healthy one; for Drum and Dance Saturday and the larger community that gathers there knowing that at any moment the numinous gateway may open; Bonnie Devlin, sage, seer, friend, Huntogi drum master who fanned the early flames; Tracy Vernon, priestess of the dance, beloved friend, for many fits of ecstatic laughter; Britt Howe, gifted shamanic artist, for her creative spirit and passion for our endeavors; Arana, for his unwavering support in the work and homestead; Matthew Blais, fellow ecstatic spelunker and magical partner; my friends and adventurers at Waking World; Orren Whiddon for his nudge off the cliff, and the staff at Four Quarters Farm for hosting some of the sweetest fire circles; Zo Carter for love and energy down the home stretch; Owen White, soul brother and coconspirator, who opened the door wide to a new level of sacred languaging and dreamtime adventures; my women's magical group, The Seven Sisters: Morwen Two Feathers, Lori Rowan, Camilla Parham, Carla Hughett, Amy Anderson, and Kathleen Chapin-Exar, gifted creators of healing ecstatic space; my family for their never-ending love, support, and encouragement of the odd one in the tree; my respected spirit teachers; and to all those I have ever and will ever drum and dance with, with physical bodies and without. Together we create the golden womb where the true magic comes to life.

1 Entering the Circle

The shaman travels lightly. His (her) most powerful tool is the condition of willingness, practiced with discernment.

Circle of Shaman

NORMALLY, I LIKE BIRTHDAYS. Even my own. In early September 1989, a week before mine arrived, I received a call from my friend Rya Penington, a gifted clairvoyant and colleague I had met through the mediumship development group at the First Spiritual Temple a few years before. Mediumship is the more classical form of the activity popularly referred to today as "channeling," a subject I had been studying since 1975. Essentially, this is a telepathic communication process with disembodied beings called "spirits."

As the development group came to a close, Rya and I and two other friends from the group, Carole and Kay, began extending our mediumship work outside the church. We offered private counseling and healing sessions to groups and individuals, which were usually a synthesis of evidential mediumship, intuitive counseling, and the healing practice of laying on of hands. We also offered public evenings of spirit communication in the homes of friends and acquaintances. These events combined lectures, demonstrations of evidential mediumship, and general question-and-answer sessions on spirit communication. The evenings were well received, and soon we found ourselves managing a backlog of requests for others.

Rya and I would get together regularly and spend an afternoon or evening honing our skills. We often used a collaborative approach in which we'd enter into a brief meditation together and when one of us received some information or image, we would share it with the other, then the other would place herself in the scene to receive additional information spirit might want to pass on. The results were always interesting and fruitful.

On this particular night, Rya was calling to invite me over to her place the following week, as she and spirit were planning a birthday celebration for me. She wouldn't share any details, but she did mention her excitement that spirit was eager for her to include a mediumistic reading for me as a gift.

At the time I gladly accepted. When the appointed day came, however, I was withdrawn and depressed for reasons I couldn't quite put my finger on. I was not in the mood to visit Rya, or spirit, never mind celebrate my birthday with them. Many times during the day I searched for a good reason to excuse myself from the commitment and just stay home alone in my sullenness.

I dragged myself there anyway, dogged by a bedraggled state of mind. When I arrived at her apartment, it was obvious to Rya that things were not well with me. Concerned, she asked about it. I slowly poured out the contents of my funk, confiding to her the strong desire I had to just stay home, admitting how hard it felt to be there and to be at all sociable. A part of me secretly hoped that she, upon hearing this, would call the evening off, or at least reschedule it. Yet there was another part of me that I knew had delivered me to this moment with a power of its own, despite fervent protests going on elsewhere inside.

After I was done venting, I paused, anticipating the reprieve I desired. Rya sat back and sized up the situation—for all of maybe two seconds. Good friend that she is, she assured me that my internal state of affairs was just fine with her, and she and spirit had every intention of going ahead with the celebration they had planned. "But first, let me finish getting ready, and I'll see you in five minutes." She headed for the bathroom.

I knew it was my last chance to escape.

I came close to getting up and bolting out the door before she returned. I couldn't believe it myself, but I was just not in the mood for any of this. But I forced myself to stay, using the some-what dysfunctional reasoning that if I left now, I'd feel guilty on top of it all for disappointing her and those in spirit who had planned and were attending this affair. Blah! I closed my eyes, took a deep breath, and planted myself in the overstuffed chair. There was no way around it. I'd just have to bear the displeasing reality of myself as the most dubious, disgruntled, disrespectful guest of honor I'd ever seen. And if that wasn't bad enough, I was acting that way in the face of all I considered sacred.

Rya returned, smiling and absolutely radiant in a colorful caftan and complimenting turban, perfectly suited for the occasion. I sunk lower into the chair knowing what I dreaded was here. Without a word she went around gathering her healing stones, lighting candles and incense, and then put on some quiet music made especially for relaxation and this sort of work.

We began.

"Lately spirit's been inspiring me to begin this way," she said as she massaged cool cream into the sole of my right foot. I saw the wisdom in this, for after a few minutes the obsessive mood viper which had coiled itself around my brain began loosening, ever so slightly. I felt a channel opening between my head and chest as if to allow the rest of my body to wick off some of the distress besieging my mind. I slowly began to relax.

With my inner eyes I watched as negative feelings rose up, one by one, from the horizon of my subconscious into the sky of my awareness. When they reached a point equal to that of the midday sun, they'd stop and hover, then slowly melt away as if caught there in an invisible beam of healing. Then the next ill feeling would rise up to the same point in the sky, reach the beam, stop, then slowly disperse into the environment. No matter what came up from the shadowy depths, the beam drew it forth into the sky, caught it there at twelve o'clock, and worked its gentle magic. As this continued for the next ten or fifteen minutes, the distress and anxiety I felt were slowly transmuted to a much more calm, receptive state of mind.

Not long after, Rya announced the arrival of my primary spirit guide, Running Wolf, a Native American man who often travels with a white she-wolf. Tonight he was traveling alone. I could see him in my mind's eye and began to place myself in the scene Rya was describing. After offering birthday greetings, he informed us he was there to introduce me to someone else. With this, Rya began seeing images of turtles. I saw them too. I was looking into layers and layers of turtles hovering before me, the mosaics of their upper shells facing outward, toward me.

After a few moments the shells began fading and a man walked forward from among them. Rya saw him at the same moment I did, "I'm aware now of another spirit who is joining us," she said.

"Yes," I broke in, "I see him, a medicine man."

Rya paused, then said, "The name I'm getting is shaman." This was probably the second or third time I had ever heard the term, and frankly, I did not know what it meant. I had sensed before that a shaman was akin to a medicine person, but her response made a firm distinction between the two.

After gifting me with a medicine pouch that had a few special items in it, the shaman proceeded with a message for me. He said that this birthday represented a rite of passage for me—that my life would soon look nothing like it had up until this point in time. As he gave me this message through Rya, I received a vision of a great vista of rolling hills and meadows that stretched out to a magnificent horizon far off in the distance. The first golden rays of the morning sun crested over the land sending ripples of color in my direction. What lay before me was a whole new world. I was both excited and intimidated by the unfamiliar expanse. I paused, then slowly stepped over the threshold into it. Not long after, the shaman departed and Rya and I brought our session to a close.

It was then midnight. I left Rya's and arrived home an hour later, where I was greeted by my bleary-eyed mother. My mother is never up at that hour and I was afraid some calamity had happened. "Rya's on the phone for you, but I don't think it's an emergency. She says she has something important to tell you."

I picked up the phone to Rya's apologetic voice. "I'm so sorry to have woken your mother; I didn't realize it was so late." She went on to tell me excitedly that after I left she had gone to bed and found herself pondering over the images of the turtles. She had the nagging feeling there was something about them we had missed.

As she reflected on this, someone in the spirit realm interrupted her thoughts and she received a message to look it up in the book. Suddenly she remembered that she had recently bought a copy of the Native American *Medicine Cards*, and dug up the book to see if turtle was listed there. Indeed it was. And the medicine of turtle had everything to do with the bad mood I was feeling earlier that night. Some of the words were even identical to mine when I was describing to Rya feeling terribly ungrounded and wandering around in the darkness, having lost my center.

It's not unusual that more information from the spirit realm comes through at a later time like this. I was impressed by the shaman and the way he worked. I realized there was a deeper meaning in the symbology he offered, but he didn't point it out to us directly at the time. We called him Turtle Man. I decided to go out the next day and pick up a copy of the *Medicine Cards*.

Even though the session I had with Rya and Turtle Man had been extremely beneficial and noteworthy, I felt no inclination at the time to research shamanism. Over the years I had come to meet many helpful spirits with a variety of interesting vocations or specialties, but had never felt prompted to delve into any of them. And so it was with Turtle Man and shamanism.

About a week later Rya and I met again to do an absent healing session for a friend of ours. As we settled into our meditation, Rya noticed a Native American man had joined us. As he came into my view I saw him to be a fairly large man who sat off to the side of us, smoking a pipe. He had his eyes closed and seemed to be praying intently. A raven was with him, and as the smoke rose from his pipe it traveled through the ethers to the friend we were praying for. The raven left the Native American man and flew with the smoke, as if guiding it to its destination.

We saw our friend sitting in a room filled with blue light and the smoke came like a mist and enveloped him. The raven lighted on a perch. It leaned toward our friend, its iridescent black eyes surveying the healing work taking place. Seemingly satisfied, it cocked its head a bit and softly ruffled its feathers. I had never seen a raven display such care and gentleness before.

When our work was finished the smoke and raven left the blue room and returned through the ethers to the Native American man who still sat cross-legged in silence off to the side of us. A few moments later Rya inquired of me, "Does the name Circle of Shaman mean anything to you?"

"No, I can't say that it does," I replied.

"Well," she continued, "I'm being told that the man praying with us is another shaman, and that he and Turtle Man are part of a group of individuals in spirit who go by the name Circle of Shaman."

"Hmmm . . . that's very interesting," I mused, as I began to suspect something unusual going on.

Following this message, we received a kind of dictum from this group, of which we both received pieces. Putting them together resulted in this message: "The shaman travels lightly. Her (his) most powerful tool is the condition of willingness, practiced with discernment."

Our session ended soon afterward. Although no other information was given about this group, both Rya and I felt that there was an alliance being formed between us. We were amazed as, over the next few days, we came across information in the *Medicine Cards* that corroborated key aspects of our experience with the praying shaman. We read that smoke is considered to be visual prayer in many Native American traditions. In addition, the raven, with its ability to navigate through the Great Void, is frequently associated with absent healing. Once again, the deeper symbolism and meaning of our work with these two shamans was impressed upon us. At the time of our absent healing session, we had no idea of the significance of smoke or raven in healing work.

A couple of weeks passed and the next time I entered into this work was at home by myself, the night I met Grandmother Illusion.

It was a warm October evening and I had just settled down to begin my regularly scheduled absent healing meditation. As I followed the drone of crickets deeper into the sacred zone, I encountered her, this elder shamaness, the one who would be called Grandmother Illusion. The one who would turn my world upside down.

I could see her clearly in my mind's eye. She appeared in simple clothing: a cream-colored skirt with a shawl wrapped loosely over her head and shoulders. Bent over with age and ancient wisdom, she moved about slowly and deliberately, as you might imagine a dignified elder would. She was crouched close to the ground, her wrinkled hand drawing symbols in the sand with a stick that had a few leaves attached at the end. She turned to me.

"Shamanism is evolving," she said, and then paused. "Evolving to a form never before seen on this planet."

Her message, spoken with few words, took me aback somewhat, for at the time I had no idea what shamanism was—never mind how it was or was not evolving. Yet a vague feeling of recognition or remembering reverberated through me, sending a chill up my spine as she made me privy to her thoughts. Since I had been involved in the study and practice of mediumship for many years, I had come to meet many people from this other realm, so her appearance along the inner path of my meditation was not unusual or discomforting in and of itself. But still, her message was a bit unsettling. Why would I be told such a thing?

I sensed that my primary task there was to listen, and I offered just one response during the meeting, after she informed me that shamanism was evolving. I thought to ask her why this was so. Her poignant, albeit understated, reply was, "Because the needs of the people have changed." With this she returned to silence and her artwork in the sand. A small crow had perched itself comfortably on her shoulder and together the two seemed completely absorbed in her work.

I was curious as to what she was drawing, and she didn't seem to mind my inquiring eyes, so I looked down into the sand before her. Her central symbol was a circle and, one at a time, she was adding lines that stretched from one point in the circle to another point, seemingly arbitrarily. For some reason, watching her drawing this made me think of the Earth.

As soon as I had this thought, my field of vision was filled with a three-dimensional image of the Earth floating before me in living color, though the color was dull. As I observed the image, everything about it spoke feelings of fatigue, congestion, disease. Soon strands of light began appearing, one after the other, connecting one point on the planet to another, just like the sand drawing Grandmother Illusion had been making. These strands increased in number, forming what looked like a web of shimmering light and color encircling the Earth.

I was told that each strand of light connected shamanic individuals across the planet, one with another, whether they were recognized shamans by vocation, or just those who, knowingly or not, lived and worked in a shamanic way. As I watched, the light within these strands grew brighter, and with it, so did the colors of the planet.

Suddenly one of the strands lifted out of the vision and attached itself to me, and I was no longer observing the image. I was in the image, a part of it, and able to perceive myself as both the point at the end of a strand, and as the entire web itself. In those few moments, I felt the growing brightness of the web in my own body and the birthing of new strands, as if they were my own. It all seemed to be occurring from the information and energy being shared collaboratively along the web, and also more than this.

As this sharing took place, the web became not only invigorated, but excited in an emotional sort of way. The web felt clearly to be a living, sentient network, I would almost say "being," that I was and was part of. I also felt the intimate connection the web had with the Earth, and how through this communion an incredible regeneration of life energy was happening. This transformation seemed all one seamless, organic process with no clearly distinct origination point, and it was breathtakingly beautiful to watch and feel.

A few moments later the strand dislodged itself from me and the vision came rapidly to a close, which was probably a good thing. Although my body was tingling all over, I realized I was in way over my existential head—there was much more information in these sensations than my rational mind could comprehend. Then Grandmother Illusion appeared once again working at her sand drawing, the crow still perched on her shoulder. As if the vision wasn't overwhelming enough, I also had to fathom another tidbit of information. Grandmother Illusion turned back to me once more and added, "You have a role to play in this process. You are to write a book about it." As the imagery quickly faded, Grandmother Illusion also departed, leaving me with these words: "You know all you need."

I was dumbfounded.

It took me several minutes to recover from the shock of this experience. When I did, I wondered if I had really seen and heard what I thought I had. I considered the few words she had said. What puzzled me most was not so much her message that I was to write a book, or that shamanism was evolving, but rather her last cryptic statement that I know all I need. I know all I need for what? To write a book on shamanism? That hardly seemed true. Was it merely a rhetorical statement, a mystical koan of some sort? From my sense of her, that hardly seemed true either. So exactly what was it that I knew?

On the surface, what I knew from this meeting was that something about shamanism and this evolution she spoke of was related to the experience of this living web. A web that connected all shamanic peoples and seemed to have a capacity to bring new life and vigor to the Earth and to the people. And I was supposed to write a book about it—a subject I knew nothing about. Yet the words of Grandmother Illusion implied differently. Did I know something I didn't realize I knew? And if so, how could I discover, or uncover, this knowledge?

I felt my soul responding to this call, this challenge, despite the bewilderment and chagrin of feeling unwittingly swept up into the clutches of a larger story—a much larger story than the one I'd been living for thirty-six years. Body humming and head spinning, the urge to enter the dreamtime came over me early that night. I found myself reflecting over the sequence of events that led me to meeting Grandmother Illusion in the first place, and the group she hailed from, the Circle of Shaman. Perhaps I'd visit the bookstore tomorrow and see what I could find on this thing called shamanism.

"I'm looking for books on shamanism," I said to the crystal-adorned woman behind the counter. She pointed to an aisle on the other side of the store as she answered the phone. I wandered over in that direction and came upon the shelf I was looking for. "Shamanism" the label read over a shelf that overflowed with books on the subject. A wave of nausea overtook me. I did my best to ignore it and scanned the shelf to see if I was intuitively drawn to any of the volumes stacked there, an approach that tends to work well for me.

The books stared blankly back at me as if asking, "So? What do you want us to do?" I felt nothing, save the uncomfortable protests of my stomach. I tried picking up a book or two at random and read through the table of contents, but found I just couldn't focus my thoughts and comprehend what I was reading. Perplexed and a little aggravated, I moved away from the shelf and noticed the nausea slowly began to subside.

Curious, I made my way to the door and the welcome fresh air. Thinking it just a fluke, I went to another bookstore around the corner to check out their books on shamanism. The same thing happened. Normally exceptionally healthy, I wondered if perhaps I was coming down with some kind of intestinal bug.

I waited another week and tried again, with the same results. Every time I approached a bookshelf holding my potential treasure trove of research books, I would start to feel ill. It was as if there was an energy deliberately repulsing me. I was back at the first bookstore and the crystal-laden woman I spoke with the week before saw me puzzling over the books.

"Are you interested in shamanism?" she asked, apparently not recognizing me.

"Well, yes, actually I am," I replied with some hesitation. I went over to the counter where she was taking care of some paperwork.

"Then you should come to this weekend's workshop on how to become a shaman," she said, glowing. My stomach turned over. In my travels I had begun to notice the many ads tacked up by people offering workshops on shamanism. I looked them over, rationally and intuitively, but none appealed to me, and in fact, I had begun to suspect that I was knocking at the door of some New Age fad. The plug from the sales clerk, although well intentioned, helped to drive home this feeling and did not help my nausea at all.

I thanked her for the recommendation and bustled myself back onto the streets of Harvard Square. I felt sick, confused, frustrated. I began to doubt the message I had received from Grandmother Illusion, from whom I hadn't seen or heard since— not that I had tried to contact her. I confided to my friend Carole what had happened when I tried to look into books on shamanism, and that my initial sense of it was that it was just a fad, therefore something I had no intention of wasting my time with. I vowed to never get involved in anything like that, while she nodded in sympathetic support.

I began to put away my desire to continue a deeper investigation into shamanism, surmising that the message I received a few weeks ago had been a mistranslation on my part, at least the part of it where I was to write a book on the subject. Even if it wasn't and the subject was not simply the current New Age trend, how was I supposed to research the topic and write about it if I couldn't even pick up a book without being overwhelmed with nausea? It made no sense to me. On top of this, Rya and I had met a couple of times and practiced our mediumship work without any further visits from the Circle of Shaman.

Unable to figure out how to proceed around the riddles that lay before me, I shrugged the topic off, although something still nagged at me. I had a vague suspicion that I was missing some key piece of information. But what, and why? In my meditations later that night I prayed to be clear enough to receive and recognize any guidance spirit might be trying to give me on the issue. And if truth be told, I secretly scanned the places I went for the next several weeks, to see if I could detect a shaman among the many people whose paths I crossed on the streets, in cafés, and at bookstores. I also indulged myself in a romantic fantasy that one would recognize me as a sincere and worthy student and we'd have some kind of fortuitous meeting, but no such thing happened.

2 Encounters in the Dreamtime

Old Man said to the people: "Now, if you are overcome you may go to sleep and get power. Something will come to you in your dream that will help you. Whatever these animals tell you to do, you must obey them, as they appear to you in your sleep. Be guided by them."

Blackfoot Lodge Tales

WHEN I MET GRANDMOTHER ILLUSION and the Circle of Shaman I had begun deliberating my retirement as a medium, or at least taking a long sabbatical. Even though I had been working successfully with it and I enjoyed working with others in this way, for years I had the feeling I was meant to either do something more or something different with these skills than working as a spiritual counselor and evidential medium. Which is not to take anything away from the field. I found it to be rich and full and extremely beneficial in many ways. I simply knew it wasn't quite my path in life. I knew this even when I began my mediumship training, yet I also sensed it was an important stepping stone of sorts to this elusive "something else," whatever that was. After my vision of her, I found myself returning to these thoughts and preparing to make a decision, and as I did so there was a growing feeling of despair that began to settle around me. I began to withdraw from people and activities that had given me much joy and satisfaction over the years. I felt nervous and irritable a good deal of the time, for no apparent reason.

It had been a few weeks since I had meditated or tried to contact spirit, and I hadn't felt much desire to, but one night as I settled in to read for the evening, I felt a strong inspiration to pick up a little frame drum I had and drum. I knew this feeling. It was a kind of tap on the shoulder I'd receive from spirit when there was work to be done. I was surprised in a way, because I'd felt so out of it lately and couldn't imagine what "good" I could do in my general state of befuddlement.

I picked up my drum and began a monotonous beat on it. After drumming for a few minutes I began to feel bored from the monotonous rhythm and wanted to do something more creative, but try as I would, I simply could not break out of the repetitive pattern. Finally I just settled into it and let myself go. I wasn't thinking of contacting spirit, I wasn't thinking of my melancholy, I wasn't paying attention to what I was doing. I just let the drum take those thoughts away. It almost seemed as if I were following a protocol, or knew intuitively what to do; but whatever it was, it didn't resemble anything I had learned in my training or work as a medium.

Suddenly, with my inner senses I felt fingertips at my lips, and it was Grandmother Illusion! She had something in her hand that she wanted to put in my mouth.

"What is this?" I asked her, as I felt her fingers deftly deposit some kind of roughage on my tongue.

"They are dreaming herbs; plant spirits and crushed crystal together. You need to take close note of your dreams," she replied matter-of-factly.

"But, there's so much I need to ask . . ." I entreated.

She ignored my plea, yet not without compassion. "Keep drumming while you hold these herbs in your mouth. Let them dissolve slowly with the steady rhythm of the drum."

I sensed I was in the hands of a master, and as best I could, trusted that intuition and kept drumming. I soon found myself going into a trancelike state, and I didn't resist. I just let myself go as I had before. No thoughts. No feelings. I just let myself slip into this void, a void I could feel was alive, a void that, after a few minutes, emanated a faint chanting, as if somewhere off in the distance just over an invisible hill there was a circle of tribal peoples whose chanting reached my inner ears. The chanting wove and curled itself around the monotonous rhythm of the drum.

One of the things I discovered during my mediumship training is that most mediums receive information clairvoyantly,

which means "clear seeing." Clairvoyants are those who receive
information in visual images. Another way of receiving information, although not as common, is *clairaudience*, which means "clear
hearing." Mediums who work with clairaudience often receive
messages with their inner ears, as if listening to a spirit voice speaking to them. The third faculty for receiving information is referred to as *clairsentience*, or "clear sensing." This faculty tends to
be more amorphous and impressions a bit more difficult to articulate because they are absent of images or words. Many mediums use all three faculties to receive information, although there
is usually a predominant mode they gravitate toward.

For me it was clairsentience, the most challenging one. It took
me a long while to learn how to grasp impressions and render
them in ways I could then relate to the sitter. With clairsentience
the medium is often directly in touch with a spirit communicator's
emotional reality.

My big breakthrough came one day when I realized that the
reason I could not get a clairvoyant read on the spirit I was com-
municating with was because I was actually inside of him looking out through his eyes. Once I realized this, I began to receive
more visual impressions from this perspective. I also began to pay
more attention to the kinesthetic impressions I was receiving, for
they were laden with information, though not available to me
through the more customary visual or auditory images.

As I attuned my perceptions to these kinesthetic impressions, I
could feel such things as the spirit's height and weight in my own
body. I could feel if they were thin, or heavyset, or muscular. I
could feel, as I said, their emotional reality, including what felt to
be their intentions. So when I was visited by Grandmother Illusion, I sensed her primarily clairsentiently. It was through this sensing
that I felt her compassion toward me. I also felt her expertise and
mastery that lay far beyond my ken. So putting my trust in her was
not quite a matter of blind faith. I did have something to go on.

I had also come to learn that important messages from spirit are often revealed over time, which challenges the credit-card mentality I was prone to at the beginning of my training. The American way is to see something you want, and take this little piece of plastic into the store and poof, you go home with a new possession. It doesn't work this way in matters of the spirit. It doesn't work this way at all. That was something I learned early on, for which I am grateful, because this realization enabled me to cultivate a level of faith and patience I hadn't known before and am still building upon today.

Finally, some time later, the rhythm of my drum and the chanting released me from my entrancement. I looked at the clock and was surprised that only thirty minutes had passed. I could've sworn I'd been drumming and listening to chanting for hours. "This drumming is pretty powerful stuff," I thought. "I'm going to have to check it out someday."

I went to bed that night with a notepad by my side.

Although I woke up the next day not remembering any specific dream, I did have several over the next month that were unusual. In them I met with other beings and they taught me things, although I couldn't always bring back the details intact. Sometimes these teachers took human form, and other times they resembled mythical human-creatures of some sort. One of these dream teachers took the form of a large hawk with the face of a man. This hawk-man flew down from a tree and visited me. We had quite a long and pithy conversation, although the details remained in the dreamtime.

During one such dream, one of the first, I became aware that I was visiting with a humanlike being and it became a lucid dream of sorts. As we were visiting together, I recalled the problem I'd been having with nausea whenever I went to pick up books on shamanism, so I decided to bring this question up.

As I raised the issue and began explaining it, this very intense wave of nausea came over me and I could not continue my conversation. My companion did not seem to mind and patiently sat with me for a few minutes, but the nausea didn't pass. "I'm afraid I'm going to have to go," I said to him, as I felt I was on the verge of losing the contents of my dream stomach. But he held my arm and motioned another humanlike being over to us.

I was not at all happy with the notion that my audience was growing.

The next thing that happened was beyond my sensibilities. This other being came close to me, face to face, and moved to put his mouth upon mine.

"Oh no, no, you don't want to do that!" I protested as vehemently as I could. But the first being was persistent, assuring me that both of them knew fully well what they were doing. I finally gave in ambivalently and let this being place his mouth on mine.

With that, my stomach released its vile contents and I could feel this other being drawing it into himself. I was totally repulsed by what was happening, but the first being continued to assure me that all was well. As I surrendered into the experience as best I could, I had the very clear intuition that this was an act of love and beneficence that these beings were expressing to me, the power of which brought me close to tears in their presence.

There was a lot of sickness inside of me. The second being kept drawing it out of me into himself. When the foul liquid was gone and the being took his mouth away, I looked down and noticed that I could see inside my body. What I saw was a large crystal inside my abdomen where the sickness had been. I couldn't tell if the crystal had been buried beneath the sickness all along, or if these beings had somehow placed it there once the sickness had been removed. Either way, they weren't telling me. For days afterward I could actually feel this crystal inside me. It was shaped like an L with the long taper resting against my right side pointing up, nestled against the bottom lobe of my right lung.

Another unusual pattern during this time was that I would have dreams within dreams; again, usually involving meeting different beings. When I was in a classroom situation with one, I found myself taking an impromptu field trip of sorts, falling asleep in class and going off to visit another teacher. When that visit was over, I woke up back in class again with the first teacher, feeling a little guilty I'd gone off like that, but it never seemed to bother the teacher or anyone in class. Who knows? Maybe I wasn't the only one taking these little field trips. Maybe what appeared as the classroom was actually a cosmic train station.

As I reflected on the fragments of these dreams during the day, I could often feel the presence of Grandmother Illusion. Every once in a while she would interject something, usually on the nature of illusion and darkness, which is how I came to call her Grandmother Illusion. She advised me to think about illusion as the process of truth that evolves over time. Illusions are akin to stepping stones that usher us into deeper awareness; a feedback mechanism by which consciousness grows and develops.

She told me, "The universe wastes nothing. Everything has its purpose, even darkness and illusion."

One day as I was reflecting on one of these instructional dreams in which she had played a role, I felt her presence. She prompted me to pick up a pen and write. As I did, I felt her hand guiding my own and the following story emerged. In retrospect, it is a composite of a few of the dream journeys and waking meditations involving Grandmother Illusion.

ENCOUNTER WITH THE DEMON

She quickly entered the dreamtime and soon found herself walking along the path that led to the elders' lodge. As she approached she wondered what her time with the elders would bring. Perhaps it would simply be a pleasant visit together, huddling with them by the fire and listening to the old stories and laughing with them . . . or crying. Or perhaps she would learn more about dreaming herbs this evening from the one she called Grandmother Illusion, an ancient but very adept shamaness who spoke quietly and with few words.

She arrived at the lodge, lifted up the hide covering the door and stepped through. To her utter surprise she was not in the familiar lodge of the elders that she knew so well. She turned around abruptly, only to find that the doorway she had just passed through was no longer there.

Instead of the gentle fire in the center, the familiar faces of the elders, and the quiet murmuring of their voices, she found herself in a silent, dark, and shadowy place. Where was she? What had happened?

"Be cool," she thought. "Think."

Suddenly she recalled Grandmother Illusion telling her that the teachings were being given to her for an important purpose and someday she would be tested on them. This test would involve her entering the Second World and meeting a demon there. That's all she was told. A chill coursed her spine. She sensed intuitively that this was the test Grandmother had spoken about. She quickly reviewed everything she had been taught about the nature of darkness and illusion:

Darkness is not an evil place; it is a place of birth, death, and rebirth. It is a place of immense power—and alchemy. It is a vortex that connects one directly to the Great Void, beyond even the place of the Great Mysteries. There are many beings and creatures who make the darkness their home . . . including the demons, or those that some might call evil.

But these demons, Grandmother had told her, are akin to an old snake who has refused to shed its skin in order to grow. It clings to its old ways and habits, resisting and refusing the natural flow of its own evolution. The old skin begins to distort the life force within it, and as a result a condition of toxicity begins to grow that affects the entity on many levels.

Fear, however, fear of growth and evolution comes to feed on this toxicity, this poison, which can easily become a satisfying meal. It brings comfort to the demon. Unlike love, however, this comfort is not self-renewing. The fear must constantly be fed for the toxicity and comfort to be maintained. This is the demon's focus, its raison d'être. It survives upon fear and the toxicity the fear is fed by.

And demons have insatiable appetites. In the Second World, demons have the ability to detect and merge with fear in others, as quickly as a shark is drawn to blood in deep oceans. With the knowledge they gain from merging with another's fear they can manifest themselves in a variety of forms, until they find the one that evokes the most fear, making their next meal as tantalizing as possible.

She turned around slowly. Her heart was pounding. She noticed a heavy grayish-brown cloud hanging in the air not far away. It began to roll around and ominously change shape with every thought and feeling she had.

The cloud gathered and condensed itself into a tall column before her. Soon orange eyes began to appear at the top—four of them. A head took shape beneath the eyes, like that of a hideous gargoyle, and horns sprouted from the top and sides of it. A grisly mouth slowly gaped open revealing razor sharp fangs. The rest of the column became a serpent's body that slowly began to writhe and twist around itself as if strangling unseen prey.

She had been taught well, but had never encountered a demon such as this. This was the Second World. There was no sound here. Her skin felt no warmth or chill against it, but rather it prickled beneath the surface on the inside. Deep inside her she felt as if every organ in her body had swelled to twice its size with adrenaline, and there was a dull throbbing ache through her entire being.

She felt the demon beginning to seek out and merge

with her fear and she thought to fight it, but as she did its eyes only glowed brighter. Because she was an *empath*, she was able to shift her attention and invoke those abilities, but they told her nothing more than what she already knew. She called out in her mind to the elders, to Grandmother Illusion and the Great Spirit, for their assistance, and the demon chortled. It had sensed not so much the details of her call, but the growing desperation in her being. Yes, this was just what the demon was hoping for: to sweeten the pot with desperation.

Through her empathic connection she became aware that the demon was deliberately taking its time with her. This one enjoyed torturing its victims before striking. It opened its mouth wider and two more rows of razor sharp teeth appeared.

It was the teeth that scared her the most. She wanted to turn away, to close her eyes and just not see them. But she knew that that would only freeze her in her terror, one of the things the demon was eagerly trying to achieve. At the moment she closed her eyes or turned away, she knew the demon would strike its lethal blow. No, she would continue meeting its stare. As long as she kept her fear in balance with the rest of her emotions and it did not engulf her, she would survive.

If she could only not see that gaping mouth with those fangs, it would make her task so much easier. And what was her task? Her task was to simply get out of there alive. . . .

"Face your fears. You *must* face your fears!" she had been told by more than one elder. "You are not just your body, or your thoughts, or your emotions. You are spirit and you must be willing to die—to let everything else die that is not of the spirit."

Yes, that was the key! She was afraid to die. She had felt her task was simply to get out of there alive. Until that thought changed, until she was willing to die, she knew she would remain face-to-face with this demon for a very long time.

She realized the demon knew her fear was beginning to stabilize. It swayed ominously, and then leaned in and she felt another surge of its energy merging with her, even deeper than before. "NO!" she shouted inside. In that moment her fear spiked and the demon opened its mouth wide and reared back to strike.

As the demon committed itself to this action she suddenly realized that she was in power. But what could she do? As the gruesome mouth opened wide before her and the demon hurled itself toward her, she decided that if she was to die she would make it the best death the universe had ever seen.

Somewhere in her being came a word that Grandmother Illusion had spoken many times before: surrender. But what did it mean? There was not enough time to think. The teeth came rushing toward her. Spontaneously she flung her arms open in a wide embrace and in a voice that rang out clear across the world of shadows she proclaimed to the demon and to all who would hear, "I am spirit!"

The last thing she saw were the demon's eyes and a look of astonishment and confusion etched across its face. In the next instant its teeth gnashed through thin air and its body burst into blue and purple flames.

Then it was silent once more, and the shadows slowly swirled and danced in the darkness.

It was then about six months after my first meetings with Turtle Man, Grandmother Illusion, and other shamans from the Circle of Shaman. I was learning that each of these spirit people had a certain specialty, and different ones appeared as I engaged in different types of spiritual healing. Although Grandmother Illusion was my more regular visitor from this group, there were two others who made occasional visits. One was a man who appeared regularly whenever I drummed or used my rattle, which I had begun to use in facilitating healing with others.

I recall the first evening we worked together. I was going about my mundane business, doing laundry and other sundry chores, when I suddenly felt summoned by spirit. This didn't happen very often, and when it did, there was always an important reason for it. So whenever the call came as clearly as it did on this night, I would do whatever I could to accommodate it. In less than ten minutes I had retired to my room, and lit the candles and some sage on my healing altar.

As I finished my preparations, I sat back and began entering my familiar meditative space, where I was soon greeted by Running Wolf. He informed me something "new" was going to happen this evening. He then introduced me to another spirit person, a man who did not appear to be Native American, but I believe was indigenous to the Asian continent—Siberian or Mongolian, I felt. This man instructed me to pick up my frame drum to provide drumming for a healing ceremony that was about to take place. Everyone was waiting for me. So without further delay, I retrieved my drum from my altar, settled myself again, and began to drum the monotonous rhythm I'd become accustomed to.

As I did so, I was transported to a little village somewhere in a sparse, steppelike countryside. I could feel a chill in the air and a sense that I was at a high elevation. Soon, images began to form for me. There were simple tents pitched here and there in a circular formation, and I could see smoke billowing gently into the sky from a fire that felt to be central to the healing ceremony. My perception was strange in that it seemed I was looking in on the ceremony as if from a distance. And yet I could also feel that I was not on the periphery of this affair, but integrally woven into the fabric of the healing circle, a circle that I felt had many participants, perhaps twenty-five or so. I was not accustomed to working in a group this large. This was indeed a new experience.

As I began to join my thoughts with this group and its intention, my awareness of myself as an individual began to disperse. I found it difficult to focus and keep my consciousness attendant to the task at hand. In the past, whenever I had participated in absent healing, I would hold the person attentively in my mind with my thoughts and prayers, and oftentimes infuse their aura with various shades of color and light. When I felt the light body respond in some fashion, whether I saw or felt it sparkle or glow brighter, it was generally my cue that the healing had been received and the time was drawing near to depart.

But on this night the rhythm of the drum carried me deeper into a trancelike state, I simply could not stay consciously aware of what was transpiring in this healing ceremony. All images faded away, but before they did, I thought I saw someone who looked vaguely familiar to me, someone I knew here in physical reality, being brought into the center of the circle. I tried to maintain my attention, but to no avail. Then I struggled with the concern that I was failing the group in some way, and the person needing healing by not being fully present and working the way I usually did.

The shaman who ushered me into the healing ceremony appeared and pulled me out of the circle for a private message. "Look, stop struggling. Do not worry about what you used to do. This is different. You are not the only one doing the healing here. Your role is to drum. And it's important, for the drumming will help bring forth the healing that is required. Let your thinking go. You will be guided through other means. Simply trust and follow the drum."

I understood what I needed to do, and frankly, I was relieved. I thanked him and we returned to the ceremony. I slowly surrendered to the drumming, letting it carry me deeper into the ceremony and into the one mind formed by the prayers and intentions of the circle.

All images ceased. The rhythm on the drum was monotonous and hypnotic. It fluctuated somewhat, but to no great degree, as energy waves and pulses moved through me from the group. The drum seemed to mark these waves, as if sending out a beacon of light, illuminating the path of our travels. It also felt to provide a certain kind of focus for the healing energy that could then be directed by those doing the actual "hands-on" healing. A few minutes later, even these impressions were lost upon me and there was nothing else I was aware of but the voice of the drum.

Sometime later my conscious awareness began returning, and I was told by Running Wolf that the ceremony was drawing to a close. I opened my eyes and glanced at the clock noticing that twenty minutes had passed, though it felt like a much longer time to me, not that I was tired. In fact I was energized.

The image of the tent village returned to my mind's eye and the spirit-people who had participated in the ceremony seemed to be returning to the places they had been summoned from. The shaman I was introduced to said I had done well and indicated that there would be other opportunities to heal together through the use of rhythm. I nodded my interest and appreciation. I felt the now-familiar energetic signature of another one from the Circle of Shaman.

From this point on, integrating drums and rattles into my meditations felt to be a natural aspect of healing work. Sometimes people requested me to work with them in an absent healing way, and when I did I always included the drum. During many of these occasions the Asian shaman would appear and oftentimes he would present me with a symbol or an image while I was drumming, with instructions that I draw it and give it to the person I was praying for. The symbols never meant anything to me, and I was never sure they'd mean anything to the people I was drawing them for, but I was surprised time and time again as they did. So drawing these images became another aspect of my practice that I incorporated with the drumming.

Although I still could not pick up a book on shamanism without feeling nauseated, I had over this period of time begun to feel comfortable working with the various members of the Circle of Shaman through my dreams and meditations. I didn't worry about books and I received no further inspiration from the Circle that I needed to focus on them, so I let it go.

As I continued to work with the Circle, I became aware of something—a desire, a purpose, or a plan of some sort, in which it seemed they were endeavoring to either create or expand upon a circle of shamanic people to work with. I had the distinct impression that there were other spiritual pilgrims like myself with whom they were already working. Feeling unclear about this purpose, I began to think about facilitating a group of like-minded people that would meet on a regular basis to explore the relationship between drumming, meditation, and healing, and the ways they might contribute to improving the health and well-being of ourselves and others.

But as I began to put these plans together, they felt somehow premature or off the mark. Although I did not carry these thoughts out any further at the time, I could feel that there was something about the general idea that was correct. If the Circle of Shaman had a charter, there was an article that addressed the need to form a closer working alliance with a physical circle of shamanic practitioners in the physical world. There was no doubt in my mind about that. How it was meant to happen, the form it would take, and my role in it, were much less clear. During this time I periodically returned to the vision of the Earth cradled by the living web of people sharing shamanic knowledge and energy and communicated my openness to bringing this vision about to the Circle of Shaman and Greater Powers listening in.

I continued using the drum and rattle in my private meditations, and in the summer of 1990, I had the opportunity to experience the profound power of rhythm in a group setting. It was August and I had invited the members of an esoterically inclined cyberspace community I was involved with to a gathering at my home. It was a warm, sunny day and several people had arrived from different parts of the country, some having never met face-to-face. There was much frivolity in the air amidst tarot cards, astrology charts, and conversations about earth changes, crop circles, and other subjects both sublime and purely mundane. The atmosphere was filled with a tranquil yet electrifying presence.

Although it was evident that my guests were enjoying themselves, I was pestered by an increasingly anxious, nervous kind of energy. For a while I shrugged it off as emotional jitters due to hosting such a large event, hoping in the back of my mind that I was doing it well enough so that my friends and guests were feeling comfortable and having a good time. Since everyone apparently was, and this nervous feeling continued, I found a quiet nook outside by a bright spray of daylilies to spend a few minutes to myself.

There I closed my eyes and checked in more directly with this energy to try and discern what it was about. As I did, I saw Running Wolf and other spirit people drumming and dancing with great vitality, and they were strongly encouraging me to bring this idea to my guests. I had not experienced drumming and dancing with a group before, but from what I was seeing in this vision, Running Wolf and his companions were extremely excited about the prospect of this, and since I had invited people to bring musical and percussive instruments with them I thought it'd be a great thing to try.

It was now dusk, and I began to filter through my guests telling them, "There's going to be a drumming circle in thirty minutes, and whoever would like to take part, please come and bring instruments if you have any. And if you don't, no problem, there'll be extras to share."

A half-hour later there were a dozen or so people with an assortment of drums and rattles, and I forget now how we actually got going, but it didn't take much prompting. Someone started a rhythm on a frame drum and, one by one, others quickly joined in; some using rattles, others chanting, some just swaying to the rhythm. Not long after, perhaps ten or fifteen minutes, it was apparent that we had all entrained together and had entered into a group trance of sorts. Everything that happened from there was improvised in the moment. People drummed, rattled, chanted, and moved freely. Few, if any, words were spoken.

I began receiving a communication from an elder Native American man who spoke to me about how difficult it was for him as a visionary in his tribe to see the coming decimation of his people. He had a hard time reconciling how to carry this vision and why he would see it in the first place, because he was only one man, and what could one man do in the face of such a vision? This was a challenging communication for me because I could feel his pain in carrying such knowledge, although I knew what I felt was only a sliver from the depths of despair that he felt.

In the meantime, my friend Carole was receiving the image of Running Wolf, dressed in white buckskin with the wings of an eagle and he was going around the circle dancing in front of each person in turn, offering a simple message as to why he was here with us. I later captured the essence of this drumming evening and Carole's impressions with the following poem.

The Eagle's Dance

As the prayers of our drums
invoked us into sacred space,
another circle,
faint at first,

emerged from the ethers
around our own.

Figures soon became visible.
Women and men, young and old.
Faces of brown, red, yellow, and white,
Feather headdress, carved staff,
white robe, wooden mask.
We recognized
through inner sight or sense
the familiar essence
of our guides and teachers,
those who walk with us in spirit.

From this outer circle
came a Native man
dressed in white buckskin.
His arms were the wings of an eagle;
the golden eyes and curved beak
resting over his crown and third eye.

They began, eagle and man, to dance
the eagle's dance
to each drummer in turn.
"Summoned by your sojourn's call
we have come to dance you awake,"
the man would say
in a direct, yet humble way.

With those words, the essence of his spirit
and that of the great winged one
entered into our beings,
borne through the ecstasy
of their dance and our pulsing rhythms.

And in those sanative moments, this we knew:
that our spirits joined not only
with the man and bird
and those in the outer circle,
but also with the Earth and heavens;
and seeped deeper still
into the web of all our relations—
with the Great Spirit in all things,
and we became one.
And in that world among the worlds,
secrets of an inner universe
were made known to us.

And so it was, as it always has been,
and always will be,
that spirit comes to awaken us,
soaring upon the wings of rhythm,
encircling our forgetfulness
with the rapture of being alive
in the temples of our bodies
at the altars of our souls
in the bosom of Mother Earth
here and now.

This experience with the drumming circle proved to be very powerful for everyone. Carole and I were inspired to go around the circle offering healing through the laying on of hands to whomever wished it. It was not quite clear how long we drummed and chanted that night, but it was probably two hours or so. The energy drew itself to a close, and afterward most of those who participated said they wanted, even "had to," meet on a regular basis and continue drumming together. Eight of us did so for about a year, meeting approximately every other week. We referred to ourselves as the Arcana Drummers, in honor of the name of the cyberspace community in which we had met. It was during this time that my fledgling love affair with drumming began to crane its neck over the edge of the nest and look out, wondering what great world lay beyond.

3 Awkward Awakenings

Which would have the greater effect in your life: my compassion for you or your compassion for yourself?

Running Wolf

The plunge within is the way of the shaman.

Stephen Larsen

The task is to go deeply as possible into the darkness…and to emerge on the other side with permission to name one's reality from one's own point of view.

Anthea Francine

DESPITE REGULAR MEETINGS with Grandmother Illusion and other spirit allies that unfolded into sublime experiences through meditations, the dreamtime, and now rapturous drumming, I found myself with an ominous incongruity on my hands. As these bright mystical interludes became more frequent and profound, an equally profound and spreading darkness began to encroach upon me.

This dichotomy slowly rose and loomed like a sharp blade over my existential neck. I felt I was the object of some kind of cruel cosmic joke. For everything I had come to discover and know about myself during the preceding fifteen years was now being stripped away by an unseen hand, slowly, resolutely, without pity or compassion. The more I fought or resisted or tried to intervene in this process, the farther out into the desert I seemed to wander, increasingly more lost than found, the blade never far behind. I struggled with a growing sense of impending doom as I tried every way I knew to reconcile or stave off this dark numinous force. With each failure I felt myself lapsing further into a double life.

"What the hell is going on?" I would moan. An insight I had gained over the years would come to mind—that my transformational process was cyclical in nature and each cycle, no matter how dark, had eventually given birth to greater understanding of myself and my world.

"Trust the process," I'd coach myself, waiting as patiently as I could for the dawn, (which I hoped was just around the corner). To my dismay I found such invocations impotent against the advances of this shadowy transgressor.

The very core beliefs about who and what I was, about what I had discovered and culled from the last decade and a half were now under siege. I had felt quite content, inspired, and well adjusted . . . up until recently. Although there were still periods of inspiration, I was no longer content or well adjusted. The image of the person I knew myself to be lacked its former solidity. But what was causing it to disintegrate? ·

I examined my life thoroughly, looking for clues. There were none, save the fact that this disturbing darkness began around the time that I first met the Circle of Shaman. That such intense discomfort could be related to such sublime experiences was a paradox incomprehensible to me, and so I dismissed any connection between the two. It was increasingly difficult to hang in there in the face of the despair and meaninglessness I encountered, and almost impossible to "trust the process," whatever process this was. The words that had been so vital and inspiring to me in the past now rattled together like dusty old bones. It was almost impossible to trust anything anymore.

One night when I felt somewhat calm and lucid, I offered the following reflections to my journal.

I'm consumed by growing anxiety and darkness. My nerves are on edge. I look in the mirror and do not recognize the person looking back at me. Who is she? She seems so strange. I'm taken by spells of dizziness. Not just in my head, but from deep within my body. My mind wanders, intent on divorcing itself from me, and in the process produces a most uncomfortable disorientation, as if becoming entranced by this strange upsetting force against my own bidding, and certainly against my better judgment.

I look around at my surroundings, the place I grew up, and it seems so peculiar, like a foreign land, as if I'm just a visitor here in this body and time and place. Something is dying, and I am stuck somewhere, in between the worlds of life and death . . . a psychological purgatory. I don't know what's going on or why. I don't know what to expect. Once in a while I get a glimmer that it's positive, but a moment later I doubt this feeling, totally convinced I'm simply deluding myself. The existential ground I've spent so much time getting solid beneath my feet is crumbling away and I can't stop it!

My fears come and devour me, like hungry vultures. I'm trying desperately to keep up a persona that everything's okay, but it's not. I find it difficult to connect with others, even those who've been close to me. I tell myself the connections are still there, and I believe it, to some extent, but it's almost as if there's a barrier, a thick film, distorting my perception, preventing me from seeing or feeling them. The greatest safety and comfort I find is simply in being alone, and sometimes I feel I could get through this if only I didn't have to deal with the outside world. I long to immerse myself in nature and promise myself to take a retreat soon.

I don't know what kind of help to ask for or from whom. I don't know how to describe what's going on, and worse, I can't figure out what the hell is causing it! Difficulties and dark times are no stranger to me! But never have I felt so raw and vulnerable. What professional therapist would hear of these experiences and not think me crazy? Talking to spirits! Surely a therapist would insist that I take some drug to remove these vultures and subdue the visions themselves that are about the only thing that give me solace! What is this terrible vexation and why is it imposing itself on me?

Back in Harvard Square one warm summer day, wandering around the bookstore, I found myself drifting over to the area of books where I typically felt nauseated. I hadn't given much thought to researching shamanism over the past several months. I walked over and began to scan the books. No nausea. Whoa. I remained there for a few minutes feeling just fine. I was excited by the possibility of being around shamanic literature without feeling ill. I slowly walked away to absorb the novelty of this experience, to acknowledge the potential turning of a new page in my quest and actually to see if there was any pulse left in the quest.

As I walked around the bookstore beholding this revelation, the vision Grandmother Illusion brought to me of the sickly Earth, the living web of shamanic peoples infusing it with vitality, and the message that shamanism is evolving returned. A feeling, a desire to renew this quest, slowly began to rekindle itself as if leaning against a smoldering coal. It *was* still alive.

As I turned and headed back over to the bookshelf, I fantasized going home with at least one book on shamanism and wondered how I would choose from the proliferation of titles on the subject. Maybe spirit would draw me to what I most needed. I sent out a silent call and invitation to my discarnate allies for their help. I spent several minutes scanning the volumes. Still no nausea. I was elated, although none of the titles impressed me. I paused to consider my options.

Out of the corner of my eye my attention was drawn to something on the floor to my right. I looked down and I saw the word *Shaman* in white letters against a dark background hovering above a man in colorful ceremonial attire with eyes closed. I could have sworn this book wasn't here a minute ago. If it was, how could I have missed it? I half-smiled to myself, suspecting this to be the sign I was looking for. I picked it up with a silent thank you.

I gazed at the cover and noted the full title: *Shaman: The Wounded Healer*. The author was an anthropologist by the name of Joan Halifax. Something about the subtitle, "the wounded healer" sent a shock through my system. As I thumbed through the slim, richly pictorial volume, my eyes began to fill with tears and my legs started to tremble. I put the book under my arm and hastened to the checkout counter and out of the bookstore. I didn't even bother to check for other titles. I could not wait to get home and explore what felt to be a newfound passageway into a world I had wanted to peer into for almost a year, and had almost given up for naught.

I could not wait to make the forty-five-minute trip home and it was a warm day so I headed for my favorite spot down by the river. Once settled, I wasted no time meeting the wounded healer. In the very first paragraph I discovered that the vocation of the shaman has ancient roots that predate the earliest recorded civilizations by several millennia. Then I came across my first clue of profound portent—a sentence that caused me to immediately sit up and take notice. Although the role of the shaman has taken many forms throughout time and he or she lives at the heart of some cultures while on the fringes of others, "Nevertheless, a common thread seems to connect all shamans across the planet."[1] Once more the vision of the living web connecting all shamanic peoples across the planet loomed brightly before me. I found the correlation of the message in my vision with this statement to be a very intriguing "coincidence."

As I continued to feast upon Ms. Halifax's treatise, I noticed a strong and repetitive emphasis was placed on the word *myth* and variations such as *the mythic realm* and *the mythic imagination*. Apparently, shamanic work was performed in the mythic realm, and the otherworldly journey the shaman took to this place was done by invoking the powers of the mythic imagination by establishing an altered state of consciousness. As I read, spellbound, I realized that there was a breadth and depth I had never known or suspected in relation to the term *shaman*.

I also noted that the shaman often uses various forms of rhythmical expression to achieve an altered state of consciousness. While these forms include such things as singing, chanting, and dancing, I was astounded to discover that the drum shows up as the primary vehicle used to alter the shaman's consciousness in many cultures around the globe. In such cultures the shaman has an intimate relationship with this instrument. I thought back to the

encouragement I had received from some members of the Circle
of Shaman to incorporate the drum into my healing meditations.

In particular, I thought of the evening Running Wolf had
introduced me to the Asian shaman and how I had been instructed
to drum that night for the healing circle ceremony. How I had
struggled with this way of healing and the Asian shaman pulling
me aside to remind me that I wasn't the only one doing the healing, and that my role there was to drum. Could it be that I was
drumming for him, or perhaps others to journey that night for
the person who was brought into the center of that healing circle?

As I continued to read I discovered some striking similarities
between my work as a medium and that of the shaman. We both
seek counsel with those who exist in nonphysical forms and realms
in order to help others. Another curious resemblance is that while
the shaman employs the services of a helping spirit, which often
takes the form of a power animal, I had the same kind of relationship with my primary guide, Running Wolf, who often travels
with a white she-wolf. (Was she his power animal, I wondered?)

I was inspired to follow these threads and others that Ms. Halifax
brought to my attention. Within a week I had six other books on
myth and shamanism, by authors such as Joseph Campbell, Mircea
Eliade, Roger Walsh, Michael Harner, Gary Doore, and Stephen
Larsen. My pioneering spirit in full flight, I began staking out this
new territory. The following summarizes what I learned.

Although there is considerable variation in perspective, most researchers agree that shamanism is a very complex system of traditions and techniques that focus on diagnosis, divination, ritual,
healing, and empowerment, and is oriented around the extensive
use of altered states of consciousness.

The definition of a shaman offered by Harner[2] is, "A man or
woman who enters an altered state of consciousness—at will—to
contact and utilize an ordinarily hidden reality in order to acquire

knowledge, power, and to help other persons. The shaman has at least one, and usually more, 'spirits' in his personal service." Eliade[3] refers to the shaman as a "technician of the sacred," for he or she is one who travels between the sacred and profane worlds via this altered state of consciousness and seeks to heal afflictions of the soul. The ability to travel in this way is referred to as "journeying" or the "flight of ecstasy."[4]

Shamanic figures in European Paleolithic cave paintings date back at least thirty thousand years, attesting to the ancient roots of shamanic tradition;[5] and it is a practice found across the globe, not only in Europe, but also in Asia, Africa, North and South America, and Australia.[6]

My research also revealed that shamanism, in fact, is considered to be an important precursor to the world's great religious-spiritual traditions.[7] At this point there is no evidence of any other spiritual tradition that predates shamanism.

Although shamanic rituals and practices differ widely from culture to culture, the underlying archetypal aspects are remarkably similar, not only cross-culturally, but also across the millennia. This common archetypal thread, woven throughout, bears undeniable testimony to the power and mystery that lie at the core of the shamanic experience, and even more so, to the power and mystery lying at the heart of the human psyche itself.[8]

Historically, the shaman's role has always been to help ensure the survival and well-being of the tribe or community. The shaman accomplishes this by being a link, a nexus, between the sacred and mundane worlds. This link is established by the shaman's ability to induce an altered state of consciousness and enter the sacred realm, a reality ordinarily beyond that of waking consciousness. There the shaman receives or gathers information and then must return to disseminate it to the community in such a way that it is useful and beneficial to human affairs and activities in the profane world.

The shaman journeys in order to learn, to heal, and to help. He may seek knowledge, and power either for himself or for his people. He may seek information for healing, for hunting, or to appease and petition the gods. He may also retrieve the souls of the sick or guide the souls of the dead to their eternal resting place. Hence the shaman is frequently referred to as a psychopomp, a guide of souls.[9]

The shaman has three basic responsibilities: the first being to ensure a connection between the ordinary, profane world and the sacred world; the second, to lead the tribe in applying its mythology to new situations and circumstances; and third, to assist the tribe in transforming its guiding mythology when it fails in helping them to adapt to new situations.[10] The shaman assumes the role of a public servant, and sacred action is directed toward the creation of order out of chaos.

Today, as the majority of the world has become industrialized, one of the shaman's primary roles is no longer as essential as it once was—that of summoning beasts for a successful hunt. The shaman, however, remains the mediator between the mythic world and ordinary reality. "He is the prototype of the artist, the priest, the dramatist, and the physician, all rolled into one."[11] Although shamans are and have been many things, they are, above all, healers.[12]

Everything I was reading about shamanism told me it was a way of knowing, of healing, and of transformation used by many tribal cultures, past and present. As I probed deeper I was astonished to discover that the major archetypal themes of shamanic initiation brought an exceptional level of clarity and coherence to this recent transformational phase I had been struggling through—an understanding I had long been seeking, but had not found. What a relief to find some evidence that the psychological territory I had been groping around was familiar to many people in many cultures, both present and past—

for thousands of years—and the process was familiar as well.

As I delved incredulously into this information with one "ah ha!" after another, I began to wonder why I had been kept from it for so long, being overcome with nausea whenever I approached volumes holding such precious knowledge, volumes holding the answers to so many questions I had pondered. Why was I not permitted to discover these things almost a year ago when Grand-mother Illusion and the Circle of Shaman first approached me? What or whom had stopped me? And why?

I found a clue in reading about shamanic apprenticeship. I learned it's a process that may vary in length from a few days to years, depending upon the culture and type of service the sha-man will be performing. In some cultures, an elder shaman as-sists the initiate in getting in touch with his or her own helping spirits in nonordinary reality and then departs, apprenticeship lasting no more than a week. This is especially true of the Shuars, who live in the Ecuadorian Andes.[13]

More importantly, once a person gets in touch with the spirits, there is no need for a physical mentor, because the spirits supply the answers. The real teachers of the shaman instruct him or her from the sacred realm. There are no other higher authorities.[14]

It suddenly dawned on me that my rational approach to this had been all backward. Since the ultimate teaching relationship for the shaman is through her connection with helping spirits, then the absence of an elder physical shaman to instruct me now seemed both reasonable and plausible. Perhaps my nausea was a reaction to help ensure that my relationship with the Circle of Shaman, my helping spirits, would be solidified first, before I became influenced or diverted by other sources of information. Intuitively I began to sense that the Circle of Shaman and my own greater spirit had orchestrated events exactly as they had occurred, in the specific timing, arrangement, and flow from one to the next, including the nausea to ensure this connection.

Although I had gleaned that the nature of my involvement

with Grandmother Illusion, Turtle Man, the Asian shaman, and other members from the Circle of Shaman over this past year was about establishing a working relationship, what I didn't realize until this point was that they had also been instructing me about shamanism. To me, our work together appeared to be an extension of mediumship, which in many ways it was. I had no idea that the heart of shamanism was this intimate working relationship with the shaman's spirit helpers. Scattered pieces of the puzzle that had been presented to me during the past year started to fit together.

While I found an immense relief in discovering this information and could appreciate the metaphysical poetics of it all, my exuberance didn't last for long. Other deep-rooted questions soon arose: "Why had I, a modern-day Western woman, a former yuppie who had come of age in the hippie generation, come to be unwittingly, spontaneously, and irretrievably engaged in something that so closely resembled an ancient primitive initiation process? Was there some relevance, some connection between my life and shamanism? And furthermore did a more-than-casual connection exist between the world of the shaman and the contemporary industrial world I knew so well?

Everything I was now unearthing and its implication to the recent events in my life intimated that the answers were "yes." The question of my personal involvement was, of course, the most mysterious to me. Was it to write a book as Grandmother Illusion had mentioned in our first meeting? And if so, was it a necessary prerequisite to experience these acute psychodramas and have my life literally turned upside down to do so? Or was it more than this, a purpose that was as yet unrevealed?

I considered these questions in light of my new information, noting how the turbulence and teachings over the past year closely resembled some of the dynamics found in a shamanic initiation crisis—not that I necessarily believed I was being initiated as a shaman, but there certainly was some kind of intense transformation going on. Although the answers to some of my questions were sequestered somewhere in the folds of my soul, and, I suspected, in the overarching purpose of my connection to the Circle of Shaman, I did recognize two things quite clearly: I had become involved in something much more capacious and complex than I had ever imagined, and it was no fad.

4 Dark Night of the Soul

Our task is to cross the thresholds
into unknown lands
where our teachers
may provoke our initiation
and our demons summon our illumination.

May the Great Spirit smile within us
making our spirits strong
and our souls light.

And what we learn, may we carry it back
whole or in part
and share it with our village.

Nadu, Circle of Shaman

Within the shamanic initiation experience,
a harmonization of the spiritual, social, and
natural worlds takes place. The emergence
of new forms of global culture depends upon
this harmonization.

Rowena Pattee

I N October of 1990, a few weeks after my introduction to the wounded healer and after mulling over some of the similarities in my own life, I experienced my first "official" drumming journey. It was an evening when the Arcana Drummers had gathered and Penny, who had been studying shamanism, offered to lead the group to discover a power animal in the way she had learned. I later learned that this type of drumming journey is a common introduction to many contemporary forms of shamanic practice.

Even though I was feeling a surge of the general anxiety I'd felt over the past year, I figured I'd have no problem with the exercise. The directions seemed clear enough, and since my childhood I'd always felt an intimate connection to nature and animals, even to the point of considering the woods my first home. I thought the journey might even offer a nice respite from the anxiety, as well as opening me to another spiritual resource. It opened me up alright, although it was far from the respite I had hoped for. An entry from my journal describes the experience.

By the light of candles and the scent of burning sage, we settle back comfortably and listen to Penny as she begins drumming a monotonous rhythm on her frame drum. I soon find myself entering an altered state of consciousness.

Following her guidance I look for a hole in the earth. I find one at the gnarled base of a great oak tree. I travel easily past root and rock and the tunnel opens up into another place where a bat soon greets me. It hovers and darts about in a playful sort of way. Our eyes lock for brief instants as it spirals in close, then flies out of sight and returns again. It reveals itself to me three times in those first few minutes; therefore, I accept it as an authentic power animal according to the instructions Penny had given to us before we began.

The imagery suddenly shifts and I find myself in the middle of an intense interdimensional storm of some sort. All I can see is a brilliant red sky lighting up in flashes all around me and there is a terrible wind whipping at me as I struggle to walk along the path. This path winds and twists, traversing a steep mountain, the edge of which disappears into a deep, dark gorge. Another mountain shrouded in darkness rises up on the other side. Flashes of lightning in the sky make it more visible. The winds are so strong they nearly tear the clothing away from my body and I have to clutch them to me as the wind begins to shred them. I struggle to keep walking and not be blown over.

The awareness that then comes to me is that symbolically, my ego is being stripped away from me. As I am having this thought I am asked a question by some unseen being:

"Are you *willing* to go through this process?"

I think about this question for a few moments and then have to answer honestly, "No, I am not willing to have my ego stripped away." The same question is repeated to me, although I don't feel pressured or that my answer had been unsatisfactory. After a few moments I still have to admit to the same answer—"No, I'm not willing to go through this process."

I begin to wonder why I am expected to answer, "Yes, I am willing," anyway, because if I am meant to go through the process of having my ego stripped away, I believe my soul will see to it that this would happen, so I, the ego-me, don't have to say yes. It also seems ridiculous to think the ego-me would say yes to its own death anyway. Of course it wouldn't be willing! Satisfied with the seemingly sound logic of this conclusion, I determined that the question was, somehow, irrelevant.

Wrong! As if someone had been listening in on my thoughts I am told, without delay, that I do have to answer, "Yes, I am *willing* to go through this process." (There is a strong emphasis placed upon the word "willing.") I listen to this with respect, but it still does not make much sense to me, and if the truth be told, it does not change my answer. I mentally communicate "I still cannot answer yes," to this unseen being. The journey ends shortly thereafter with the bat flying directly toward me with its mouth open and teeth bared then penetrating deeply into my heart. I feel a sharp pain in my chest as it enters.

As I was going through the journey, I was aware that a part of me did not trust the information I was being given about the question and the necessity of a "yes" answer. So before the journey was over the unseen being informed me that I would have a series of irritating experiences over the next few days, such as stepping in gum, and they would be a sign that the information given to me in the journey was true.

During the entire drumming journey, I felt emotionally detached, psychologically adrift, and disconnected from everything and everyone, including the imagery that came to me in the journey. It was as if I were observing myself outside of myself at the drumming circle that night.

Well, I did have a series of irritating experiences over the next few days. (Boy, did I!) But even after two days, when I thought of the journey and the question, "Are you willing to go through the process?" my honest answer was still "no." I was also still feeling numb and very detached from everything around me. Then the next day something in my emotional state began shifting unexpectedly. I don't know exactly what precipitated it or how it happened, but I decided to go for a long walk around the Arnold Arboretum with my friend Nanci, who was visiting from Colorado.

We stopped by a large spreading tree and laid out a blanket on the colorful leaves that were even more brilliant in the warm sunlight. We talked a bit and did a tarot card reading. At some point during the afternoon, for the first time in days, I found myself feeling more connected and present. It felt like a part of myself had been off somewhere and was finally returning again.

By evening, I felt very much at peace and contented. Later I drew a bath. As I soaked and opened myself to the soothing embrace of the water, I thought of the journey and the question again. This time I found myself moved to answer genuinely, "Yes, I am *willing* to go through this process." Tears welled up in my eyes as this realization settled in. I didn't know what I was in store for, but I had the sense that major pieces of my life were getting ready to jostle around again and that this unseen being who asked the question was following the process.

I thought to look up bat in the *Medicine Cards*[1] to see if it might shed light on the contents of my journey. It did. I paused long and hard when I read that bat represented the medicine of shaman's death and rebirth. This symbolic death was meant to "break down all former notions of self." What was I in for?

Not long after this journey I had a dream. Before going to sleep one evening I had asked for help in understanding what was happening to me and what the source of my struggle was. In this dream I found myself visiting with the being who had been with me in the dream in which the crystal had been revealed in my abdomen. The dream felt like our opportunity to check in with each other again. Telepathically, this being asked me how my life was. I acknowledged my recent struggles. We began reviewing and discussing various experiences of my life over the last several years. At one point, when we reached the present time and my present struggles, he looked at me and nodded vigorously and empathetically, then gave me a word from his own language as if to articulate the essence of the experiences I was having. The word was *soma*, although I received no definition of the word directly or intuitively.

The next morning as I recalled this dream, I looked up the meaning of soma in my *Random House College Dictionary*, but didn't find the definition particularly helpful: "the body of an organism as contrasted with its germ cells." A few days later, however, I serendipitously came across the following reference to soma:

> The longing for illumination on the part of those overwhelmed by darkness opens the way, and the journey begins. The shaman and the seer drink from the dangerous cup of immortality to know death as life and life as death. What was vulnerable, wounded, is now immortalized.

> *We have drunk the soma and become immortal!*
> *We have attained the light, we have found the Gods.*
> *What can the malice of mortal man or his spirit,*
> *O immortal, do to us now?*
> *Make me shine brightly like fire produced by friction.*
> *Illumine us, make us ever more prosperous.*
> *Enthused by you, Soma, I find myself rich!*
> *Enter within us for our well-being.*[2]

These words reminded me of something extremely important about my recent struggles and emphasized what I was coming to know through shamanism. For the past year I had been overwhelmed by darkness longing for illumination and the way through was to consider that the path had been opened by the struggles themselves. In researching, I also learned that soma was a psychotropic concoction used long ago with which to journey and receive visions.

Looking at these two experiences in the light of the shamanic literature I was studying infused my life with a new degree of vitality and openness—and allowed me to sense more clearly that through the dark times and struggles there was a river of wisdom flowing quietly and steadily below the surface of the experiences I had been having.

Through my intuitive connection with Grandmother Illusion, my drumming journey with the bat, and now this dream, I turned my attention to exploring shamanic initiation in greater detail. One of the more acute differences between shamanic traditions are the ways one becomes a shaman, for there are a variety of avenues to shamanhood—sometimes several within the same culture.

In today's Western industrial world it is the opinion of some researchers that "initiation now mainly takes place on the spiritual plane. In an urban setting, for example, we do not find many other shamans 'authorized' to confer such initiation."[3] This was another piece of information that caused me to stop and ponder long, for it offered a clue as to how I might think about what was happening to me.

There are several ways one may enter into the shamanic vocation; but none is more dramatic or mysterious than the initiation crisis, a transition to shamanhood through a dramatically painful event like disease, injury, or psychological upheaval. While the call to shamanhood in dreams "can sometimes be ignored and suppressed, the shamanic initiation crisis certainly cannot. It explodes through the shaman-elect with life-shattering force, disintegrating the old equilibrium and identity and demanding birth of the new."[4]

Eliade[5] found that from a collective perspective, the initiation crisis contains the following universal themes: suffering, death, and resurrection. I was startled by the word "resurrection." For some time when I would acknowledge and contemplate the pain, confusion, and despair I was undergoing, a word often emerged in my mind as if to name what was happening: crucifixion. Yet I was not sure how this term fit because I had not been a practicing Christian for years, and I associated crucifixion with Christianity. When recalling my religious teachings, I was still uncertain as to how this word applied to my experience; unlike the story of Christ's crucifixion, what was happening to me was clearly not being perpetrated by people or circumstances outside myself, but rather by some nameless, faceless, numinous force that seemed to be working within me organically, from the inside out. And for what purpose, I didn't know.

Only later did I discover through my research that these same themes are found not only in shamanic cosmology, but also in every major religious or mythic system that speaks to the process of transformation from the profane individual into the sacred self. And then I realized how the word crucifixion fit in.

In Christianity the beginning stage of the initiatic experience is often referred to as "the dark night of the soul," when one enters into the experience of suffering. The Eucharist, when richly understood, brings the initiation experience full circle. It is the symbolic enactment of the death of the profane self and the rebirth in Christ, or the sacred self. In Tibetan Buddhism this same experience is reflected in a practice called *chöd*, and according to legend, the Buddha gave his flesh to starving animals and man-eating demons—the self-concerned person willingly dies so that a new, universally concerned person may be born.[6]

The shamanic initiation crisis then is essentially an inextricable experience of intense psychological chaos and turbulence, sometimes lasting for weeks or months, and in some cases for several years.[7] In the shamanic worldview, however, such experiences are requisite for dissolving any habitual ways of seeing and behaving that would interfere with fully assuming the shamanic vocation.

The initiation crisis also offers the initiate opportunities to discover and learn how to employ the power that exists in the sacred realm, as traditionally the shaman's intent is mastery of that power. And there is something else that the initiate comes to learn and understand first hand: life is a continual transformational process from birth to death to rebirth; the sacred wheel of life forever turns, the knowledge of which affirms the immortal spirit of the shaman and everything else that exists.

As the shaman-elect enters the first phase of the shamanic initiation crisis—suffering—a powerful and pervasive subtheme is often found—dismemberment, which is usually accompanied by grisly imagery. Through the process of suffering, dismemberment, and death, the mythic world opens up and a mystical union occurs with a sacred order of being that ushers the initiate into worlds far beyond the local boundaries of the profane world she knew so well. The Yakuts, a tribal people in Siberia describe the experience:

> They [the shamanic ancestors] cut off the [initiate's] head and place it on the uppermost plank in the yurta, from where it watches the chopping up of its body. They hook an iron hook into the body and tear up and distribute all the joints; they clean the bones. . . . They take the two eyes out of the sockets and put them on one side. The flesh removed from the bones is scattered on all the paths in the underworld; they also say it is distributed among the nine or three times nine generations of the spirits which cause sickness, whose roads and paths the shaman will in the future know. He will be able to help with ailments caused by them; but he will not be able to cure those maladies caused by spirits that did not eat of his flesh.[8]

The dismembered initiate not only dies in and of herself, but also serves as a sacrament to the spiritual forces of the universe. Is it any wonder that perhaps the deepest meanings of life and existence emerge into the consciousness in the face of impending death?

But the initiation process does not end here. The spirits who dismembered or feasted upon the initiate are the same ones who clean and replace her bones and organs and re-member her. The initiate then discovers firsthand that the same forces in the universe that come to fragment and devour her follow by healing and resurrecting her.[9]

Therefore, the motif of death is viewed in shamanic cosmology as a harbinger of transformation, an opening to greater levels of energy, power, meaning, and awareness. Death is followed by "resurrection," a return to life, a rebirth into a greater, more expanded sense of self. This initiation process allows the sacred self to emerge and assume the shamanic vocation.

The symbolic enactment of death and rebirth then, whether experienced through a communal ritual or through an enhanced state of consciousness, opens the doorway to the transpersonal, to the sacred realm of the shaman. "At that point the individual leaves behind his private life and concerns and enters a mythic, archetypal realm. And the meaning he finds there is not of social fulfillment but a deeper, more profound one: a place in a larger, eternal order which transcends his local boundaries of time and space."[10]

This point proved extremely beneficial for me as the darkness I mentioned earlier continued infiltrating my life. But now I began to behold it through the shamanic viewpoint of initiation and imagined that these same mysterious forces that were coming to devour me would follow in helping me reconstitute my self and my life. It offered some stability for me, something to hold onto, a small flame to guide me through the pain, fear, and turbulence of confronting deep and old dysfunctional beliefs.

During the next several months and years I would come to see with increasing clarity just how powerful certain fears were, in not only influencing my life, but in many cases, running it.

How cleverly and creatively certain parts of myself tried to disguise and keep this awareness away from the part of me who wanted to meet and resolve it. But now, in the midst of the confusion and struggle, I was also vaguely aware that a greater meaning and purpose were emerging from the very heart of my struggles, and that my struggles themselves were an integral part of the process. This represented an entire shift in how I perceived the process I was undergoing. I now knew that ultimately, my old sense of self was dying so that a new one might be born, and I was actually able to find some degree of comfort and even inspiration in this, where before I could find none.

The study of shamanism and its relevance to my life process intrigued me so intensely that I felt compelled to incorporate it into the degree program I was pursuing through Lesley College and even changed my major to accomodate it. There was no question now. I had to follow the path newly revealed beneath my feet.

5 | Spiritual Talismans

Ecstasy and sacrifice are shamanic experiences needed in the midst of the modern global breakdown of traditions...so that regenerative powers within us can be summoned.

Rowena Pattee

Nothing determines who we will become so much as those things we choose to ignore.

Sandor McNab

The seat of the soul is there, where the outer and inner worlds meet.

Novalis

I WOULD LIKE TO PAUSE TO HIGHLIGHT two approaches I've found most helpful in dealing with the turbulence of initiatic experiences: understanding the motif of death, and approaching life with a condition of willingness.

> Whenever a profound experience of change is about to take place, its harbinger is the motif of death. This is not particularly mysterious, since it is the limited view and appraisal of oneself that must be outgrown or transformed, and to accomplish transformation the self-image must dissolve.[1]

When such a transformation is initiated in one's deeper self, the reverberations eventually penetrate conscious awareness. They usually announce themselves by producing distress or unease in your being, either physical, mental, or emotional. Neither meant maliciously nor directed by an authoritarian godhead figure as punishment for wrongdoing, these reverberations that ripple throughout the ethers of the self serve as a call, an invitation, or perhaps what might be best described as an invocation, for the community of the self to participate in the sacred event about to occur.

When these messages are received by the ego-self however, without knowledge of the mythic pattern infusing them, a mistranslation is almost certain to occur. The motif of death accompanying these messages will oftentimes be interpreted literally by the ego-self and subsequently be projected onto the screen of the conscious mind as images of one's own impending physical death or the destruction of the world. Instead of being considered as an invocation to a profound experience of change, the death motif is reduced to expressions of pathology—something needing to be neutralized or obliterated to restore well-being.

This mistranslation can be a source of confusion and terror, for the motif of death not understood through its mythic tenure can intensify the existential issue already being debated on the ego's political platform—which is the dissolution, in whole or in part, of some aspect of the self. Without appropriate support, guidance, or intervention, this existential debate can rise to crisis proportions in which the motif of death can be projected then internalized as suicidal urges.

So it is important to remember that the transformation process always begins and is accompanied by a level of discomfort, unease, or despair, and in this case is not pathologically based, but rather is a prelude to a profound change and impending rebirth of some aspect of the self.

I found myself reflecting upon the drumming journey I had in 1990. The question I've had since then about the emphasis on the word "willing" nudged at me incessantly as I went about preparing to continue work on my thesis through Lesley College. Why was it necessary for me to be willing to have my ego stripped away?

As I contemplated this question, an insight came to me about the transformative power of willingness and with it, sacrifice, and how they are both necessary to facilitate a collaborative relationship between the sacred and profane selves.

Sacrifice in its truest sense means "to make sacred." To make sacred means "to bind back together again," to reconnect.[2] In order to create sacredness, an "exchange" between the spiritual and material realms is necessary.[3] Reconnecting these realms is the primary goal of the shaman—the exchange needed to do so is the focus of shamanic action. In order to reconnect the spiritual and material realms, a collaborative relationship between these two realms needs to be established. Both realms need to reach out to each other; some aspect of the profane self has to be given to the sacred, while some aspect of the sacred is given to the profane. Essentially, this is the goal of ritual, to make sacred by making a symbolic exchange between the spiritual and material realms. In all reality, it is this exchange that infuses the basic dynamics of transformation, both individually and collectively.

The insight that came to me revealed that this process of exchange is occurring regularly deep within the psyche—that it is an inherent aspect of human beingness. The conscious awareness of this exchange, however, tends to elude the waking mind as it is usually engaged and distracted by the daily mundane activities required by survival in the profane world.

But how much greater benefit might this act of making sacred offer if we became consciously aware of the exchange taking place in ourselves at this deep level? To become consciously aware of such a process, one has to somehow recognize when it is happening and that one is participating in it. And how much greater the potential benefit if one is not simply a passive participant, watching the "dance" from the sidelines, but actively dancing the dance oneself?

Now I understand why the word "willing" was emphasized in the question during my drumming journey. The need for me to answer, "Yes, I am *willing* to have my ego stripped away," was to evoke the conscious awareness of a sacred activity occurring within myself.

In essence, therefore, this question was actually an invitation. An invitation to participate in what is probably the most sacred act available to a human being—the conscious exchange between the spiritual and profane realms of your own being. The question "Are you willing . . . ?" is nothing less than an invocation—when the question comes, some informed energy, within and without, is trying to reconnect the spiritual and profane realms and bring it into one's conscious awareness. Shamanic energy is at work.

To accept this invitation, to actively participate in this sacred activity, there is a price that must be rendered. Sacrifice, true to its popular implication, involves a death of some sort, a giving up of something. That is the price one must be willing to pay to cross over the threshold where the immanent and the transcendent meet and mingle together: to be willing to face death again and again.

In a sense, both the sacred and profane selves must be willing to experience "death." The sacred self must be willing to give something of itself, allow some aspect to leave the immortal world and incarnate into the profane—to become mortal, willing to know death as the profane self does. While the profane self, on the other hand, must also be willing to give up a part of itself—to let it go, allowing it entry into the arcane immortal world of the sacred, while it remains behind in the profane. Yet something wondrous occurs on that threshold between the sacred and profane. The sacred and profane selves meet at that moment of truth, when each gives to the other and the experience of atonement, or "at-one-ment" can fully emerge into conscious awareness.

Looking back I realize that the greatest reason that I was unwilling to have my ego stripped away was that it involved the death of some part of me. At the time I was not ready to engage in such a transition willingly and openly. Facing the unknown of such an experience was too frightening. And there were precious dysfunctional habits I didn't feel ready to face, never mind give up. But finally, the willingness to answer and participate in this sacred invocation somehow came about; and how that shift happened, I still do not know. I think I might have been tripped into it. But that mysterious force that worked in my life that day, transforming my fear and ambivalence into a state of receptivity and willingness, I call grace. The power, elegance, and (sometimes) humor of this handmaiden to the divine is unequaled to anything else I know.

The poignancy of this insight was further impressed upon me when I recalled one of the first meetings with the Circle of

Shaman where Rya and I were told, "The shaman travels lightly. Her most powerful tool is the condition of willingness practiced with discernment." What I realize now is what truly makes a shaman what Eliade[4] calls a "technician of the sacred" is the shaman's willingness to establish connections between the sacred and profane realms, and to make the necessary sacrifices when doing so. The shaman must be willing to face death, to one degree or another, for such shamanic journeys change one and those one journeys for, in ways one can never anticipate. The shaman, in order to fulfill her role, must be willing to put aside the concerns of the ego-self and direct sacred action to address the concerns of the community and the Great Mystery that she serves.

6 The Power of Myth and the Mythic Imagination

Myth is the bubbling lifespring of our consciousness…of our highest creativity as well as our worst delusions, and the secret is all in how it is tended….The shaman is man's basic creative response to the presence of the mythic dimension.

Stephen Larsen

Myth connects and relates us to our surrounding world.

Carolyn Bereznak Kenny

WHEN PEOPLE ASK HOW to approach a study of shamanism, my response is, "Start with a study of myth," for it encompasses all the raw elements and dynamics of shamanic work throughout time and culture. Myth affects all people, not just the shaman. It exerts an extremely potent and pervasive influence in our lives. An awareness of this power and tenure enhances our abilities for self-understanding and healing, of ourselves and our communities.

Here I share some of my discoveries made through research on shamanism for my degree program at Lesley College. (I draw much of the following material from my 1992 thesis entitled "Shamanic Vision and the Transformation of the Self: The Relevance of Shamanism to Contemporary Society.") We can define myth as "an intricate set of interlocking stories, rituals, rites, and customs that inform and give the pivotal sense of meaning and direction to a person, family, community, or culture."[1] Myth tells us the way the world works and how we're supposed to relate to this world. It profoundly contours a person's self-image, behavior, picture of the world, and sense of place in that world.

A living myth is analogous to an iceberg—ten percent of it is visible, above the horizon of conscious awareness, while the other ninety percent is invisible, residing beneath the surface in the unconscious mind. According to Keen and Valley-Fox[2] more than fifty-one percent of the population are not self-consciously aware of the myth that informs their existence. This is crucial if we consider that modern psychotherapy has well-documented that what is held in the unconscious mind bears a profound influence upon one's life, belief, and behavior used to display those beliefs.

We are at a juncture in history where it is critical to discover and address the roots of our personal and social malaise. "Problems such as starvation, pollution, and nuclear weapons stem directly from our own behavior and the hopes and fears, phobias and fantasies, desires and delusions that power this behavior. The state of the world . . . reflects the state of our minds. The conflicts outside us reflect the conflicts inside us; the insanity without mirrors the insanity within."[3] The roots of our most pressing issues stretch deeply into the realm of myth and the unconscious mind, for our fears, fantasies, phobias, and desires are intimately shaped by the myths that guide our lives.

Myths are also clues to the "spiritual potentialities" of human life, the secret opening through which "inexhaustible energies of the cosmos pour into human cultural manifestation."[4] The shaman is one who learns how to willfully enter and leave the mythic world and to perform his work through the deepest recesses of the psyche. Achieving an altered state of consciousness activates the mythic imagination, allowing the shaman to engage and interact with these inexhaustible energies to effect change in the physical world.

These energies take up residence in the psyche and gather identities as archetypes. Archetypes can be thought of as personifications of our innermost potentials: good and bad, dark and light, and everything in between. "Archetypes are organs of Essence, the cosmic blueprints of how it all works. Because they contain so much, archetypes frustrate analysis and perhaps can only be known by direct experience."[5]

These archetypal energies are often perceived by the shaman as totem animals, plant spirits, or other helpers that reside in the mythic world. It was through Jung's insights into what he called archetypes of the collective unconscious that Campbell drew much of the inspiration for his own work in mythology; with these archetypal energies and identities we script and enact the myths in our lives, our deepest stories upon which our beliefs rest.

Becoming aware of these inexhaustible energies and understanding how to influence them to heal the soul is what the shaman's vocation is all about. It is also what James Hillman, noted author and Jungian analyst, refers to as *soul-making*. "Soul-making goes hand in hand with deliteralizing consciousness and restoring its connection to mythic and metaphorical thought."[6] We make soul and begin to engage in shamanic work whenever we encourage the imagination to explore the mythic realm and express the images and stories it finds there. Creative writing and artistic expressions such as song, dance, poetry, and painting tap this vast reservoir of inexhaustible energies that continually flow through the psyche.

The prolific research documented over the years by Jean Houston in the area of human potential also underscores the untapped fount of creative potentials that myth and the mythic imagination offer to our lives. "I find that regardless of the culture, people will go further and faster in developing human capacities if their training is tied to a story, especially a myth. For myth transcends and thus transforms our usual blocks and conditionings, carrying us into a realm in which these need not constrain us."[7]

One of the most provocative facts about human beings is that although the structure of the brain has remained virtually unchanged for the last forty thousand years, there has been a dramatic evolution of consciousness during this time. Biologist Lewis Thomas notes that "our most powerful story equivalent in its way to a universal myth, is evolution. For the human being language and myth-making replaced genetic mutation as the primary means by which consciousness and societal innovations are carried forward."[8] Myth is the impetus that evolves human consciousness.

Through related research, storytelling and narrative are now being considered a primary aspect of intelligence and cognitive development itself—stories are an essential way of knowing for human beings: "Making stories may, indeed, be fundamental to human thinking. The ability to comprehend a story—that is, to grasp meaning within a given context—may be more basic to human intelligence than anything measured by IQ tests."⁹

Tribal and ancient cultures have always had an innate understanding of the vital need for myth and storytelling. It was not for mere entertainment, but to pass along knowledge and wisdom necessary for the tribe's health and survival. "The ancients knew many things which they had not observed in the form of hard data. They knew things which they heard in dreams, the stories of their grandfathers, the coming of events. Myth was a reality, and ritual, a response and affirmation of that reality."¹⁰ Over the eons such cultures have ushered their myths into conscious awareness honoring the deeper world from whence they come using a variety of artistic and ritualistic expressions to transmit this ancient knowledge through generations. In some African cultures, the storyteller, or the *Jali* as he may be called, is considered more important to the society than the king.

When I came to understand the importance the mythic imagination has for the shaman, I realized that it was the same faculty I was taught to develop as a medium at the First Spiritual Temple. We began by quieting ourselves and entering a meditative state of mind; then we were encouraged to open ourselves to connect and communicate with disincarnate spirits through our inner imagery process. Inevitably, when the student confronts images and impressions in this way, one of the first questions asked is "But how do I know it's not just my imagination?", as if the imagination has no relevance in the process, or is an obstacle. The truth is that *all* inner sensing and outward expression happens through the imagery process. All of life rolls out through the numinous layers of imagination first, before it hits the streets of physical reality. It is the contents of one's mythology that inherently determines the meaning and interpretation given to the images encountered in the mythic realm.

I was inspired to examine the mythology in my own life in

attempts to understand a dilemma I'd been having through many years of my mediumship practice. Despite the many lucid visions and conversations I had had with spirit communicators, once I left such an encounter, I would often find myself looking back later, questioning the validity of the experience. The meaning and poignancy would begin to slip away insidiously and be replaced by doubt. I remember lamenting one night to Running Wolf, "How is it that these experiences did not fill me with an impenetrable, unshakable belief in the reality of spirit and my connection to the sacred world long after the experiences themselves had ended? Why did a part of me seem intent on invalidating something I knew had precious value?"

Running Wolf responded by showing me an image of what looked like a great canyon in profile. At the top where the mouth of the canyon opened to the sky was a band of color that spanned across the chasm and descended about twenty percent down the canyon walls. Beneath this band of color was a great dark void that filled the rest of the canyon to the floor. Running Wolf explained that the image was an analogy, the canyon representing my conscious day-to-day life. The band of color across the upper reaches symbolized my belief in the spirit world and how far this belief extended into my daily life. The color showed that in a small percentage of my life, my belief in the spirit world and my connection to it was solid, vibrant, and robust. From here, however, it quickly dissipated into the rest of my life as a pale mist that soon became transparent, invisible, barely leaving a trace of its existence.

This image and his message were a sobering thought, for at the time I was a medium and we were talking about the underpinnings of my craft—my own belief in what I was doing. For years I was troubled by this and wondered what I could do about it. The study of myth provided me with a guide. Writings by mythologists, such as Joseph Campbell, suggested that the way I create meaning in my life is largely influenced by the contents of my cultural mythology. When I thought about this, I realized that the cultural mythology that has been seeding my psyche since day one tells me that the only thing that is "real" is what can be measured or scientifically proven. Anything else is "just" imagination or delusion, with little or no relevance to reality.

Such an unbalanced, overrational, empirical approach to gathering knowledge is referred to as monophasic: "a society that narrowly confines experience and knowledge to a narrow range of phenomenological phases."[11] And yet studies of the psyche show that it operates in an inherently polyphasic fashion, meaning that it processes information through multiple realities and states of mind. There are transpersonal anthropologists who state that "it is quite possible to argue that failure to integrate polyphasic experience may result in psychopathology."[12] I believe this a significant part of the problem in postmodern culture.

Such a prevailing overrational, monophasic mythology offers no recognition, no celebration of mystical visions. There's no such thing as visitations by angels or instructive chats or friendly meetings with trees, birds, stones, or invisible companions. In fact it is antithetical to all such experiences, and if these events occur beyond the age of twelve, they are typically classified as a pathological condition needing some form of intervention to restore conformity to cultural norms and expectations.

While such experiences may be tolerated in the life and development of children, as emerging adults we are expected to relinquish these things as our youth passes away into adolescence. We are taught to invalidate our imagination, thereby eroding our natural healing abilities and pathways into a deeper world that nourishes the very inner core of who we are. For as children, many of us have relationships with discarnate guides and companions who are typically referred to as invisible playmates. In many cases, these companions hold our most intimate joys and travails of childhood and contribute much to our healing, psychological growth, and general well-being. Such was the case with Running Wolf and me.

While other invisible playmates came and went, he and a small tribe of native people were constant friends and elders throughout my childhood. As I grew older I began to see him as my culture instructed—nothing more than a flight of fanciful childish imagination, just a dream without substance and effect in the ordinary adult world I was growing into. Although he was my trusted confidant and companion, my loyal friend and care-taker throughout troubling and lonely times, I surrendered my relationship with him, slowly cutting the ties to my personal sacred world, having no idea of what I was doing. Or the great risk I took in doing so.

Rather than bringing my teenage problems and concerns to the woods and Running Wolf, I began turning to my new cultur-ally sanctioned companions: sex, drugs, and rock and roll, with near-disastrous results. By the time I was in my mid-twenties I found myself spiraling down through a very dark and turbulent time, which I fortunately pulled out of with the help of these same invisible friends from my childhood.

The mythic imagination is that part of the psyche that con-nects the conscious mind with the unconscious mind. It facili-tates communication between the sacred and ordinary realms providing a bridge in which the inexhaustible energies of the cos-mos and spiritual potentialities may pour forth into our aware-ness. Myth and the mythic imagination are nothing less than the living informing root of human beingness.

If it were not for the mythic imagination, neither psychologi-cal transformation nor evolution of consciousness as we know it could occur. Since the core of shamanic cosmology is grounded in this intimate relationship with the mythic realm, it seems evi-dent that shamanism has played, and continues to play, a para-mount role in human evolution itself. These insights into the connection between shamanism, myth, and evolution returned me to the initial message I had received from Grandmother Illu-sion. Could it be that shamanism was indeed evolving, into a form never before seen on the planet? If so, was there also some fundamental connection to the evolutionary leap of consciousness, a Great Awakening, being spoken about in ever-widening circles at the dawn of this new millenium?

7 The Shaman's Evolving Role in a World in Crisis

When the myths no longer fit the internal plights of those who require them, the transition to newly created myths may take the form of a chaotic voyage to the interior; the certitudes of externalization are replaced by the anguish of the internal voyage.

Jerome Bruner

In moments of confusion such as the present, we are not left simply to our own rational contrivances. We are supported by the ultimate powers of the universe as they make themselves present to us through the spontaneities within our own beings. This is the role of the shamanic personality, a type that is emerging once again in our society.

Thomas Berry

The artist of the future will be a wizard, a magician, a shaman who will use any and all media to transform the consciousness of this planet.

Victor Greentree

A s I PONDERED THE CURRENT GLOBAL CRISIS and the vision Grandmother Illusion presented me, I began having brief but clear insights that there is another purpose gathering and exerting itself behind the spreading clouds of social and ecological deterioration. I reviewed the pieces of the puzzle that lay before me and slowly began fitting them together.

The central piece depicted the shaman's role itself. Ensuring the survival and well-being of the community by maintaining its connection to the sacred world through healing and ritual. In filling this role, the shaman is typically the teacher and keeper of the myths. If there comes a time when the community's mythology is no longer serving its well-being, it is the shaman who steps forward to help the tribe revision a new, more adequate mythology.[1]

That's where we are today, it seems. Our mythology is no longer serving our well-being. We are people between stories, and the existential ground beneath us is shaky and quickly falling away.

Although humankind has always existed in the context of a global community, our collective awareness of this reality is just dawning. No longer can we afford to see ourselves naively as isolated entities, securely protected by ethnic, political, physical, or ideological boundaries. For in truth, "there are no boundaries. We are in a free fall into globalism," as the great scholar and world mythologist Joseph Campbell reflected. That's what our new story needs to address.

As we free-fall into this new awareness we subsequently find ourselves in desperate need of birthing a guiding mythology that reflects the attributes of this new world and helps us to understand not only how to survive, but how to experience health and well-being in it. We need a guiding mythology that speaks of collaborative and mutually enhancing partnerships with the Earth and all forms of life, a reality the shaman is intimately familiar with.

This need sends out an unprecedented call to shamans in every culture today, for they know that to fulfill their role for their microcosmic community, they must also consider the need for the well-being and survival of the global community. One need cannot be sufficiently addressed today without taking the other into account. On one level, this is an incredibly daunting task for the shaman, but perhaps assistance is being provided by consciousness itself.

Few people could argue that our current western mythology coupled with our technical capabilities and pioneering human spirit has played a large part in creating the global issues we face. Yet over the last few decades something else has been occurring in many postmodern societies, the dynamics of which bear a striking resemblance to shamanic initiation.

As discussed, shamanic initiation involves an extremely rigorous psychological upheaval. Among other reasons, but perhaps none more important, the intensity of it is meant to dissolve addictive psychological patterns, limited beliefs, or an overly egocentric sense of self. The primary objective is to engender a major transformation in the psyche and birth a universally concerned person into the midst of the community.

Although the most acute cross-cultural differences in shamanism tend to be found in initiation rites and experiences, the three archetypal themes of suffering, death, and resurrection are found woven throughout. As we look into our personal lives and many events in the world at large, this same archetypal patterning is discernible. The core structures of our beliefs and self-image are being torn asunder. The larger ecological and social crises have plunged us into a reality in which we must wrestle with the foresight of our own extinction. We are suffering, wounded, and alienated from Soul, and absolutely no one can heal us but ourselves. The world crisis in which we find ourselves probably functions as a form of collective shamanic initiation crisis. Other archetypal aspects of initiation also intimate this possibility.

Initiation experiences often begin with a call to power where the initiate is drawn away from the mundane world and enters the unknown, one's personal mythic realm, or what is also referred to as the *mysterium*.[2] This calling may come through a specific ritual or a family inheritance or spontaneously through an ecstatic experience, a dream, a vision quest, an illness, or an affliction of some kind that produces a healing crisis.

Often the call to power is accompanied by a sense of growing despair. The initiate may feel a deep unrest in his or her soul, yet be unable to pinpoint the cause. It is key to remember that in this instance despair is not necessarily pathologically based but is intended as a wake-up call to the inner community of the self that an initiation, a major inner transformation, has begun.

Like the tribal shaman initiate, answering this call requires one to enter the mysterium to directly confront the personal demons of fear and addiction that dwell there. The aim of this journey is to affect self-healing, gain wisdom and empowerment, and return to the community as a new person, a healed person, more whole than before.

Although the specific symbolic content and symptoms of our initiations into the mysterium may differ from those of tribal peoples (as we might expect), the process is no less profound. In fact, in some ways it may be more disturbing, for our tribal brothers and sisters have established traditions, rituals, rites of passage, and the guidance of shamanic elders for such initiatic journeys, whereas this support structure is woefully absent in our society. This leaves many, as it left me, at risk of losing the struggle with the forces that come to devour the initiate during the dark night of the soul.

This first step in separating from the mundane world can be witnessed in our society over the last few decades in many ways; one of these is the growing numbers of people questioning traditional values, both secular and orthodox, in all the major areas of our lives. Additionally, with the advent of Freudian and Jungian psychology there has been a growing interest in exploring the unconscious (the mythic realm), which has expanded into related areas such as myth and dreamwork, archetypal, transpersonal, and ecopsychology, and body-oriented psychotherapies. All serve as guides and entryways into the deeper mysteries of human existence.

Two other movements that began in the sixties hastened for many of us this turning away from the mundane world. The first was the introduction to altered states of consciousness attained through Eastern meditative practices; the second sought similar results but through the use of psychotropic plants and lab-cultured LSD. Today one can find a wide variety and proliferation of individual and group meditative practices in all major cities across the United States. There is also a maturing recognition of the sacramental and revelatory nature of psychotropic plants, which have all too often been abused through ignorance and disease.

These various initiatic movements have not ended with the passage of time, but by all appearances are gaining momentum with growing numbers of people from every walk of life. Not only has the interest in Eastern meditative practices and philosophies found a receptive home here, there has also been a growing following of many of the polytheistic pre-Christian religions, all of which, like shamanism, view human beings as cooperative partners with the Earth and nature.

Increasingly, people are seeking to experience the sacred directly, both transcendentally with the greater cosmos and immanently through their bodies and natural environment. Often these experiences are sought independently from validation or repudiation of scientific and religious dogma.

This call from our mundane focus to gain more awareness of oneself can also be found at the heart of the human potential movement. Proponents here seek what is often referred to as empowerment, to discover and live from one's authentic self, to integrate the personal ego with the true self. In essence this is an effort to bring the sacred and profane realms of one's own being into deeper communion.

Could it be that we are witnessing the awakening and initiation of an archetype, the shamanic archetype, in our individual and collective human psyche? An awakening that compels us to journey into the mythic realm to be initiated into the power and knowledge of our interconnections with all life and the deeper spiritual forces supporting our existence?

While the traditional shaman has served the healing and spiritual needs of his physical community, the shamanic archetype may be seen as serving the healing and spiritual needs of the inner community of one's psyche. This archetype seeks to heal wounds on a personal level and to bring forth a mythology that supports the well-being not only of one's inner community, but also of the earth and a global community.

The special awareness gained in journeys with this archetype needs to be codified through some creative or artistic expression for "this art is not art for art, rather it is art for survival."[3] Such expression allows a greater order of peace, direction, and coherence to emerge through the chaos and turbulence of the dark nights of the soul. The process of codifying also infuses the shamanic archetype with a spiritual energy and vitality that will help it take root in our individual and collective consciousness.

Since the shaman's primary role is to nurture the well-being of the community, a major aspect of the shamanic vocation may be to evolve into a form of spiritual midwife. In this role the shaman seeks to assist the healthy birth of this emerging shamanic archetype on an individual and global level.

It's interesting to note that many shamans who, only twenty years ago, refused contact with Westerners, today are inviting people to learn about the shaman's vocation and cosmology. The message from the Shuar shamans who work with author and environmentalist John Perkins[4] is that we are all shamans who need to wake up and remember that the world is as we dream it. If we don't like the dream we can change it. They are offering to remind us how.

Perhaps the greatest challenge for the shaman and the shamanic archetype today is to bring forth the wisdom and healing power of the mythic imagination so we can live the dream many of us dream today, that of wellness for Earth and all who live upon her. To accomplish this may require nothing less than an evolutionary leap of consciousness for humankind—a leap that ecstasy, rhythm, and myth are preparing us to make.

8 Portals of Rhythm

Everyone is dying to live ecstatically in a community where spirits and people are equal.

Arnold Mindell

The tree birthed the drum so that we and spirit could speak with common tongue.

E. Bonnie Devlin

Rhythm is the language of creation.

Charles Johnston

Music and rhythm find their way into the secret places of the soul.

Plato

OVER THE FOLLOWING FEW YEARS, my relationship with drumming, dancing, and shamanic work continued to evolve into a confluence of personal healing and what I'd call interdimensional learning, centered around the ecstatic experience.

At the time these experiences began coalescing in frequency, around 1991, I had no thought or intention of working with ecstasy, nor did I have any concept of what it was or the relationship between it and healing. Following guidance by the Circle of Shaman to incorporate the drum into my healing meditations, and with my experiences with the Arcana Drummers, I was, however, seized by the power of the drum and rhythm. It continually ushered me into an altered state of consciousness and heightened sense perceptions. In these states of being, time was bent and journeys into other realms initiated that increasingly unfolded into profound transpersonal experiences of a unitive, healing, and instructive nature.

These journeys reached beyond ordinary life into a transpersonal realm, where I was brought to another vantage point to observe and participate in the workings of my soul. I was intrigued because several elements of these transpersonal experiences evoked through rhythm bore striking similarities to many I had had studying spirit communication and working as an evidential medium. But the medium's entry point into the sacred world and the shaman's were arrived at through somewhat different means. The medium went through meditation and quiet contemplation, the shaman through rhythm and physical activity. Rhythm and dance, coupled with the initiate experiences I had been having and the Circle of Shaman's message that shamanism was evolving, compelled me to know more.

Following the formation of the Arcana Drummers, my next meeting of the healing power of rhythm occurred in June 1991. My friend Charles had gifted me with the great opportunity to spend a week at the Monroe Institute in Charlottesville, Virginia, to attend their Gateway Training program. Charles had attended this training a year or so earlier and it had an immense and profound affect on his life. The institute was founded by Robert Monroe, who, in the 1950s, began having out-of-body experiences that would extend throughout the rest of his life. In these experiences, he visited different worlds and beings and authored several books on his journeys and discoveries. The institute acted as a research lab for examining various aspects of altered states of consciousness and how they were attained. This led its researchers to working with the rhythms of brain waves and they developed a process called *hemi-syncing*, which is what the Gateway Training is based on.

The Institute's programs are oriented around a carefully designed curriculum that teaches the theoretical with the experiential, combining music, guided meditations, and modulated changes in brain-wave patterns attained through different tones being sounded in each ear through headphones. This would be my first full-blown initiatory experience with ecstasy, although at the time I didn't conceive of it as an ecstatic experience.

The following is my journal entry describing my experience at the Monroe Institute June 8–14, 1991.

> The calling of the moonless night. I step upon the dirt road leading out along the ridge. Black sky filled with two thousand stars, perhaps each one signifying a lifetime. The Milky Way stretches an arm across the sky, fingers extended. Ahead a cloud of dancing lights waits to greet me. Fireflies! Soon

they surround me, blurring the line between twinkling stars of heaven and flickering creatures of Earth. Which is which? It is hard to tell. I smile and let the magic surround me.

A shooting star streaks across the sky, transforming from solid into vapor. How long did it journey as cosmic rock through space and time before transforming itself in the very instant I look up? A million years? Perhaps a billion? Where was I then?

Deep darkness now as I continue along the ridge. A sharp rustle and heavy sigh break the sound of my feet padding along the dirt road. Adrenaline rush! Stop. Listen. Sense what is to my left. I go to the fence and look over. Forms like large rocks are etched against the hillside. Soft deep breathing and an occasional snore. Sleeping cows! I stop and rest with them. I get absorbed in the gentle rising and falling of their rhythmical breathing. A low howling echoes across the hills; nearby a night bird's song rises up from a bough somewhere in the darkened field.

The next morning we begin our first hemi-sync exercises. It'll be a long week in the Controlled Holistic Environment Chamber (CHEC) units, we're told. I look around the sunlit dining room at the strangers who smile hesitatingly, yet with anticipation, at one another. We return to our rooms, to the CHEC unit that doubles as a bed. When you get in and pull the curtain it creates a cozy, womblike environment. There are a small wall-mounted light box, microphone, headphones, and a tape recorder to enhance and record your journeys. I enter the CHEC unit, slip on my headphones, and flick the ready switch. A few minutes later our hemi-sync journeys begin.

Hours and hours it seems spent in waking dreams. A multitude of images and messages. I blank out frequently in between so the pattern that connects them remains hidden from my conscious mind. A mask maker approaches and shows me an intriguing design for a mask. I notice there are many things hanging from it—bones, feathers, stone fragments. In another dream vignette, of which the images elude me, I am told that if I desire something spiritually beneficial, to "align myself with the Twin Sisters," although consciously, I don't know who the Twin Sisters are. Now I am smaller in size and I'm whisking across the desert in an energetic bubble and I come upon Carlos Nikai playing flute by a campfire under a midnight sky. A watchful she-wolf looks down upon him from a nearby cliff. My attention is drawn away from them to a single star directly above us.

In still another waking dream, a country landscape with flowered meadows, blue sky, and lazy white clouds emerges within my abdomen. Soon it transforms to an image of the Earth floating gently inside my body. All is silent and still and a feeling of reverence pervades the air. Now I am giving birth in a place of no gravity. I feel no pain, but I see a flow of blood float out from between my legs into the space around me. I blank out momentarily and in the next instant someone is handing me a drum, a tribal drum. Is this what I birthed, I wonder?

After two days of hemi-sync journeys, I am totally overstimulated. My body wisdom guides me to go to sleep the next afternoon following an exercise—to not come out of the waking dreamtime, but to allow myself then and there to be carried into the theta and delta realm of brain waves, to a place of deep sleep. I go, gladly.

The next morning I share in the group that in the last exercise I became aware that my growing edge is transforming beliefs of being powerless. Two people respond in an analytical "fix-it" way. Their thoughts do not touch upon the central issue I am feeling. I feel somehow diminished by their well-intentioned comments. Feelings of powerlessness are triggered. Soon we return to our rooms. I try to do the next tape exercise, but I cannot. Halfway through I slip off my headphones, flick off the ready switch, and bolt out of the CHEC unit.

I run outside to the hills, to the sky and sparkling sun-light, to the trees and grasses, to swooping birds on delicate wings. I bring my pain to the Earth and heavens. I sit with the discomfort. I walk with it. My solar plexus has a knot in it, upsetting my stomach. I know I don't need to do these exer-cises or be here this week to find any answers. I know I don't need to travel out beyond the Earth's etheric envelope, or solar system, or the Milky Way to "know" anything. It's all right here—in the trees, in the flowers, in the warm breezes, in the birds' songs—in me!

Suddenly the image of the meadow landscape that trans-formed into the Earth is called up in me again. The wisdom behind this image also emerges: "Yes, the trees, the sky, the Earth, the entire universe—they're all inside me!" This was not exactly a new revelation, and yet in a way it *was* new, for I realized it even more fully than before. I cry as old beliefs begin to take their next step of alchemy within me. I wonder again, as I so often have, if there are really any new truths. I think I just remember and keep expanding upon the old ones. More tears flow. The physical discomfort begins to release itself.

It dawns on me how wondrous are the ways in which we assist each other toward wholeness. Perhaps through somewhat awkward means at first glance, but underneath, how graceful and profound this life force, this healing power in each of us really is. How graceful and profound *we* really are. Later that day, having sensed my discomfort, the two people who offered analytical viewpoints gently express the hope that their comments didn't cause discomfort and my absence from the group that afternoon. I thank them for their caring and confide that although I felt angst initially, these are the insights I received as a result. We share a long hug. All is as it should be.

Sometime later, following a discussion that touched upon time travel, I sense a female presence at the periphery of my awareness. She lingers nearby for the rest of the day, that evening, and is present when I awake in the morning. As I head toward the bathroom, I realize in one of those intuitive moments of knowing who she is and why she is here. I also realize the primary purpose for my being here in the foot-hills of the Blue Ridge Mountains.

She is my future self, although future is probably a mis-nomer. Perhaps it is more accurate to say she represents my expanded, more developed self, an aspect of my total self here to introduce herself to me at this juncture of time–space. And why? For me to know of an opportunity I have—a choice. I can choose to be wooed, to be courted by her, rather than continue to be courted by my past, my more limited self.

"Don't you see?" she said, "no matter who we are and what we do, our life, in essence, is a never-ending love affair."

"I see" I said.

"New patterns are created from this knowing," she added.

I am engaged in one of our final tape exercises. We are going to a level of consciousness we haven't been to before. We're asked to have a purpose of what we'd like to accomplish while there. I decide my purpose is to explore myself and this level from the perspective of an out-of-body experience. I also choose this purpose because in a previous exercise I was aware of two beings who were assisting me as I was trying to leave my body. They had each taken an arm and pulled gently to help me slip out from my head, but there was a feeling of suction that held me in. They coached me to envision, as clearly as I could, my hands in theirs and slipping out of my body, but to no avail.

I now arrive at the level of consciousness I am seeking. I

drift in this state for a few minutes, acclimating myself to it. I state my purpose and ask for help in leaving my body. Rather than the two beings who assisted me before, I am aware there is one with me this time. I cannot visually perceive much about this being, but I do notice a peculiar tingling sensation around my body.

Now I feel this being place what I sense are its hands upon mine which are resting on my stomach. The tingling energy increases. It enters my hands and begins to move slowly up each arm. I imagine this energy to be something like golden honey in its color and movement. It feels like the start of something big. I am gently encouraged to "Receive . . . keep receiving. Drink this energy into the center of your being." (I'm aware that this is in response to an unconscious question I had, wondering how I was doing.)

"Receive? Just receive?" I hesitate. Actually, I freeze. I reflect upon the reticence I often feel about receiving. The belief I've carried that somehow I'm not worthy and okay just the way I am. This belief usually makes it difficult to receive genuine kindness or affection without some level of anxiety attached to it. The flow of golden honey has halted and is holding at about elbow level as I contemplate the vast implications of this suggestion.

I recall beginning this exercise with the energy-conversion box, a mythic box in which I placed anything that might prevent me from achieving my objectives of any hemi-sync exercises. It occurs to me that self-limiting beliefs such as these are definitely an item fit for the box, so I affirm that, indeed, they are already in there! I leap over this hurdle and choose to receive unconditionally. Yes! I let go into the experience and receive.

With this, the golden honey continues moving up my arms very slowly. It enters my shoulders, then my upper chest. The tingling and vibration is steadily increasing with each moment. At the instant both streams of honey converge right above my heart, I suddenly burst from the membrane of my physical body into what feels like another body, but its dimensions are different. I feel it especially in my face and head. It feels as though they have changed shape. My head is wider and my face has less definition of features. Although I can feel rapid eye movement of my two physical eyes, I am also simultaneously aware in this other body that my two physical eyes have become a row of small lights in the shape of a crescent around my forehead!

The golden stream of honey now reaches my heart! Instantaneously, the stream shoots itself down into both legs and up into my head. I feel I am lighting up all over. My body quivers uncontrollably, I am hyperventilating, beads of sweat pop out of my pores. I feel the most incredible vibration throughout my being I have ever felt in my life! These sensations are the only clues that I'm still connected to my physical body. I ask for help in leaving my body completely, but the sensations only continue. The power of them thrusts my hips up. It feels like my root chakra is being sucked into an energy vortex.

After a few minutes the sensations begin to slowly subside. The closest I can come to describing them is to say they are like the most intense dose of nitrous oxide I can imagine, coupled with an electrical charge. Although I didn't leave my body completely as I had tried, I find myself beaming from the incredible good feelings and afterglow. I am encouraged to rest and relax by the being who is still with me. I do.

After a few minutes I desire to try again and ask its help. The energy begins to build, but this time it is different. It is as though I am totally enveloped in a bubble of this energy and it is being absorbed through every pore of my being. It builds with similar results, although not quite as intense, and then a few minutes later, subsides.

I rest for a few minutes and try again. The energy builds as it did before, but this time it seems to be emanating from the core of my being, from the area just slightly above my spinal column, and spanning the length of it. Still I don't leave my body. I try one more time, asking for assistance again, and this time the energy builds from the core within my body and also enters my being through my breath. Every breath I take increases the sensations within my core. The sensations within my core seem to intensify the sensations of every breath. It is extremely powerful this time. I am surprised when suddenly I feel as though I am going to have an orgasm. "Holy shit!" I gasp inside myself.

I stop just shy of orgasm as I shift my attention to the possibility of having one. Although I cannot claim any knowledge of what a *kundalini* experience is, suddenly in this moment I am informed that this is what I'm experiencing. I also know it is not a prelude to an out-of-body experience. At least not this time.

The exercise draws to a close. It takes me a long time to get up and leave the CHEC unit. When I stand and walk I feel very bouyant, physically lighter. I make my way downstairs and speak to one of the facilitators. She knows about kundalini from her counseling and research work, and, I sense, from personal experience. She smiles broadly and acknowledges the experience to be what she knows as the awakening of kundalini. We do one final tape exercise and I experience the same thing several times again, the primary difference being one of intensity. It is probably about seventy-five percent as intense this time. I discuss this experience with the other facilitator as well, but I don't feel ready to share it in the group at large.

Again I hear the calling of the moonless night. I answer joyfully and quietly slip away from the graduation party. As the darkness envelops me, I hear distant howling in the hills.

A night bird's melodic song reaches my ears now and then. As I walk along I catch the scent of cows. I go to the fence and look over, but they are not there. I expand my senses, but they do not seem nearby. I continue to walk along the ridge. A few minutes later, about a hundred yards farther down the road, I hear a low gentle snore. I stop and listen. The sound of soft rhythmical breathing reaches my ears. I smile. I go to the fence and there are the dark shapes like rocks scattered in front of me silhouetted against the hillside. I rest, embraced in the sounds around me and the fullness of the moment. A crescent moon peeks coyly over the eastern horizon.

Suddenly I am aware that the being with me during the kundalini experience was my future self. She's here with me again as I stand upon the ridge with the sleeping cows. In these moments the wisdom she shared earlier becomes crystal clear. Not only do I see my life as an intimate love affair with the universe, with the Great Spirit in all things—I *feel* it. I *know* it. The universe flows through my body and my soul. Every gentle kiss, every burning disagreement; all the joys and struggles of a lifetime are an expression of grace and devotion, a sensuous flirtatious dance emanating from the heart of this relationship.

A song of gratitude rises within me. I sing it to the Earth and heavens giving voice to all the things in my life I am grateful for. I look up into the arm of the Milky Way and trace the extended fingers with my vision. A shooting star streaks by . . . I make a wish.

I was still struggling off and on with the darkness that besieged me during that first year of working with the Circle of Shaman. My general psychological state had improved largely because the study of shamanism offered me a framework in which to view the turbulence and increasing velocity of events happening in my inner world. I entered therapy in 1991 to help me integrate these events, careful to find someone with empathy and personal knowledge of transpersonal experiences. I found this in Steven. We worked together once a month or so using music and imagery as the primary means to take readings of what was happening in my inner world.

In late winter of 1992 I began being overwhelmed once again with bouts of depression and dissociation. I drove by a spunky dog cavorting in a yard one day and found myself wishing to switch lives with him. This thought brought up a deep fatigue in my heart and a desire just to be off the planet; to be out of this body, out of this head, out of this ambiguity. I knew I was in trouble. I called Steven and told him I needed to see him as soon as possible.

We met the next day and after talking for a few minutes, me apprising him of what was going on in my life, he put on the music and I laid back, cuddling myself under a blanket. After a few minutes of resistance, images began forming from the sensations I was feeling. I saw a baby lying on her back crying in a room; distraught, disoriented, and alone. I was aware of spirit people around her. They felt her pain and carried it within themselves as if it were their own. This child had been born out of her "spiritual family" this time around in order to receive a certain set of experiences necessary to help bring forth the essence of her soul and the purpose it was to serve in this incarnation. The journey would not be an easy one, and there was no guarantee of success.

The baby was me.

That imagery began to disperse and reformed into a scene where I found myself as an adult on a mesa somewhere out in the Southwest. A magnificent hawk, soaring on the warm air currents, came and circled directly over my head. I could feel it was carrying a message for me, but at the very moment where it felt like the hawk was to deliver it, the imagery began fading away. I was not at all disappointed, however, for I was left with a clear feeling that this experience presaged an important message that was on its way to me.

I returned to normal waking consciousness and shared with Steven the visions I had had. I told him I was left with the distinct impression that I'd be taking a sojourn out to the Southwest, but added that frankly, I had no idea how I'd do it as my finances were fairly limited at the time. "But," I noted, "I feel if it happens, it'll be through rather sudden and unexpected means."

Two days later I received a promotional offer from one of the major airlines. By this time life was crowding back in on me, temporarily fogging my memory of the vision two days before. It offered a $199 round-trip airfare anywhere in the continental United States. My immediate thought was "Hey, I can do this," as I envisioned myself kicking back on a sunny beach somewhere. I began fantasizing about who I might visit and where.

The reverie of my fantasy was abruptly broken when another image overlaid the beach scene: that of the mesa and the hawk. My mood shifted to serious contemplation as I realized that one aspect of the vision had just come to pass—the means to go to the Southwest would arrive suddenly and unexpectedly. I began to make other plans. The "vacation" would have to wait.

Not long after I had settled on the date and place of my sojourn. I would go to New Mexico and spend two weeks there in May. I didn't have anyone to visit, but it felt important that I spend the bulk of my time in the Santa Fe–Taos area. I called Rya, who had now relocated to San Diego, and asked if she'd like to meet up with me for a long weekend and take part in this sojourn. She gladly accepted and we soon finalized our plans.

As I was contemplating them one night a few weeks before I was to leave, I found myself called by spirit into sacred space. I closed my eyes and there was an elder Native American man standing before me, the one I had seen at my first drum circle with the future Arcana Drummers. He simply asked me why I was going to New Mexico. In my mind I had an answer, which was to go on a retreat, a personal sojourn as I had seen in my vision several weeks earlier. But what came out instead was, "I'm looking for my spiritual family." The intensity with which this deeper truth moved through me caused me to break down sobbing.

I prepared to leave for New Mexico, half-thinking I'd move out there within a year. I felt certain that my spiritual family was there somewhere, so I also saw this as a formal step to check out the area for job possibilities and places I might live. I arrived in Albuquerque late one afternoon, spent the night, and wasted no time in making tracks toward Santa Fe the next morning. Rya flew out from San Diego and joined me a few days later for the weekend. As we pored over tourist maps and books in the little hotel room, we decided to visit Bandelier National Park. The next day we left early heading towards Bandelier, after which we'd continue on to Taos.

It was a gorgeous spring day. We drove up the highway, then turned off, driving along winding roads that brought us to Bandelier by late morning. The sunlight and blue sky framed the grandeur of the cliffs and canyons which themselves held in confidence the stories and ancient ways of a time gone by. The place was alive with spirit, and just being there I found myself opening and relaxing and connecting with a greater energy in ways I had never experienced before.

After visiting a *kiva* high up on one of the cliffs, we headed back to the east making our way down into one of the canyons. With each step it felt as if we were journeying back in time. We stopped at a sharp bend in the trail, overlooking a great gorge. I imagined we were in a time pocket, perhaps at 500 C.E. We decided to pause there for a while and give appreciation to the spirit of this place. We pulled two rattles out of our sack and with an agreement for silence for the next however-long-seemed-appropriate, we rattled and chanted and danced our prayers of honor and gratitude. About ten minutes after we began, two men came up the trail from below. Though their clothes were from a modern time, we knew they were returning from a distant time before Christ.

One of them straggled along, in some degree of obvious stress and discomfort. We didn't stop. Without words we welcomed them into this pocket of time and spirit. The first man sat off to the side, while the other who had been struggling positioned himself close to the center where we had been dancing and chanting. We had moved by now, so it wasn't obvious that where he was sitting was actually a focal point of our activity. Rya and I shared a secret smile and kept on. We recognized spirit's hand in improvising a collaborative healing space, so we gladly obliged. We opened our prayers to include these travelers along the way.

The man in the focal point looked down into the canyon, over into the waterfall whose high waters tumbled down the canyon gorge, lost in wistful thought. The other just gave his friend the calm space he needed to regroup and take care of himself. Both seemed to quietly drink in the invisible fullness of what was happening.

About fifteen minutes later, the travelers slowly gathered their things to leave. No one had spoken any words during this time. The man who had struggled up the canyon trail looked visibly refreshed. His coloring was better and there was even a slight spring in his gait. He looked at Rya and I, smiled, and his lips spoke a silent "thank you." We smiled and nodded in return, the chanting and rattling expressing our thanks.

Soon Rya and I gathered our things to leave, but first we spent another ten minutes or so in silent contemplation taking in the splendor of this place, the canyon, and the time spent here. It was late afternoon now and we languidly began to make our way back to the car, our hearts full and happy, our minds in a deeply altered state of consciousness.

Rya being as strongly clairvoyant as she is, was seeing many spirit beings along the path. I, being more clairsentient, felt the air around me thick and electrified with their presence. As we made our way along in silence, me shaking the rattle to the rhythm of our walking, I found myself drawn to a peculiar outcropping of rocks next to the trail. Rya noted some strong spirit activity happening there as we approached. As I tuned into the rocks a spirit exuding a great deal of warmth stepped out from them and approached me. I opened my arms in welcome and he in turn welcomed me. He welcomed me home. I was almost moved to tears. I knew this place and I knew this spirit from a very, very long time ago.

Rya dropped back and took the other rattle and began playing it and chanting softly. The spirit and I conversed telepathically, and through movement we shared a dance of welcome, reunion, and recollection that transported us into a timeless place where the past became the now.

What we shared there was far beyond my ability to express in words, but it was a rapture of the spirit, of the joy of returning to what I can only describe as the homeland. It lifted me to heights of being I've only experienced on very rare occasions. As this intimate communion began drawing to a close several minutes later, and I felt the spirit beginning to withdraw, Rya quietly called out to me. "Karen," she said ever so gently, "look. Look up into the sky."

There, soaring upon the balmy air currents wafting up from the mountain ridge was a hawk. I knew what was going to happen. The hawk, as if following the path we were on, flew toward us. When it was directly above me, sure enough, it halted, hanging there silently suspended in the sky for a moment, then began to spiral round as if the tip of its wing was rooted to an energy beam connecting us. It spiraled around once, then twice . . . four times all together, just as in the vision. As it did, the long-awaited message was given to me.

The message was the same one I had received with Rya three years earlier, the night I met my first shaman, Turtle Man, from the Circle of Shaman: "Your life is about to change. Soon it will look nothing like it has before." Recalling my naiveté to adequately fathom what this meant the first time, I was now a bit wiser as to the proportions it might encompass, so I received this simple but profound message with all due respect and measured anticipation.

When I left New Mexico a week and a half later, I was no longer sensing I'd be moving out there. The spiritual family I found there resided in spirit at Bandelier. Meeting them quenched the thirst of my search, although I did still have this sense that there was a spiritual family that awaited me somewhere on the physical plane. This open question didn't trouble me however. I returned to Boston feeling refreshed, inspired, and invigorated, preparing once again for some kind of major life change.

As it turned out, I wouldn't have long to wait.

There's nothing like an ample refreshing vacation, but of course that means there's a pile of mail to go through, phone calls to return, and more work waiting at the office. I returned and was inundated with all three. As I began to sort through my mail, a peculiar thing happened with one of the pieces. It was a flyer advertising a drum and dance weekend being held at a campground in Connecticut by an organization called Earth Drum Council. The flyer seemed to hum in my hands. I had no idea who these people were or what they were doing. Although African drumming and dancing was a strange and unfamiliar world to me, I knew I had to go.

The event was a scant three weeks away. I had just put out quite a bit of money for my vacation, yet knew I had to find the funds to do this weekend. The price was extremely reasonable, and with some financial finagling it looked like I'd be able to go. I called a couple of friends from the Arcana Drummers I felt would be interested in this kind of adventure. They were, but both had plans for that weekend. I balked somewhat at the idea of going alone, but realized that I had to.

Although every decision you make changes your life, there are a few decisions you make that change it radically. This was one. Not only did I meet a wonderful community of people, I came to meet the spirit of the drum that weekend in a way I had not known before. It dawned on me that perhaps this was the spiritual family I had been intuiting, those brothers and sisters who came together in community to celebrate, commune, and dance their prayers around the fire to the sensuous beat of the drum. I had come home!

Soon after I was introduced to African-based rhythms I began experiencing something through drumming that was similar to both the kundalini experience I had at the Monroe Institute, and my experiences with mediumship. Though it lacked the intense physical sensations of the kundalini awakening, I could feel the same energy being excited through the rhythms of the drum. I also began having some intense mediumistic encounters with spirits while drumming, and especially while dancing.

Over the next four years I came to share a house with several other housemates I had met through the drum and dance community. During this time I began to work closely with one of them, Matthew. We'd get together at least once a week to drum for the evening. The kind of drumming we did was what we refer to as "organic," meaning spontaneous and improvisational.

The drums we used were the goblet-shaped *jembe* and conical *ashiko*, native drums of Africa. Occasionally we used the rectangular tongue, or slit, drum. We'd also include other percussion instruments such as bells, rattles, and wood blocks, but the drum was our primary focus.

Although at the time we were taking classes working with traditional West African rhythms such as *Kakilambe*, *Fanga*, *Lamba*, *KouKou*, and *Manjani*, on the nights we'd get together, we'd spend the evening immersing ourselves in organic rhythm making. Our intent was to simply use rhythm as a way to travel into ourselves to explore and express what we found together in a conversation on the drums.

The classes assisted us by teaching proper hand techniques to begin coaxing the melodies found in hands against the drum skin, and the West African rhythms increased our fluency in the language of the drum. Although such teaching is not required to have profound spiritual experiences with the drum, what is necessary is an attunement or sensitivity to rhythm, and especially a willingness to go where it takes you.

As Matthew and I journeyed with the drum through the layers of our psyche and consciousness, we discovered a recondite "something" quite accidentally. We noticed that at certain points along the journey polyrhythmical patterns would emerge—sometimes simple, sometimes complex—and on their heels came a certain energy, qualitatively different than anything we'd ever experienced.

The energy was palpable. Kinesthetically it felt as if the air around us became thicker, as if taking on a substance that wasn't there a few moments before. It gently pressed against us, not oppressive or obtrusive, like the density of humidity. This was inviting. Caressing. Vibrating.

And it seemed this vibration effused from the center of our beings and merged with the air around us, filling up the whole room. The sense of physical boundaries separating us from our environment softened. There was a rhythmical bridge we felt connecting everything together. Time and time again we traveled across this bridge to other worlds.

We, the ego we's, were no longer directing our hands or the rhythms. In this space it was as if something else had merged with us and "it" was playing our drums, both of them together. And it felt like it was playing us—that we and the drums had become one instrument for this energy to express itself and communicate with us.

After about forty-five minutes of drumming, we'd come to a close and Matthew would move to his keyboard and let the energy continue to move through him. I'd lie down across his bed letting the rhythms and melodies of his keyboard into the deep space that had been opened inside of me. There I'd begin receiving visions, impressions, or insights about a variety of things.

Eventually I'd return to my room and record the information I was receiving in my journal. Sometimes it was a poem. Sometimes an image. Sometimes it was a shard of information about working with rhythm in a spiritual or healing way.

One night, not long after we began our weekly drumming journeys, I had finished reading *The Celestine Prophecy,* by James Redfield.[1] I was feeling the energy generated from our drumming around me in a now familiar, palpable way. My visionary centers had been opened and I was beginning to receive impressions. The word that came to me to describe this experience was Beauty. I was deeply submersed in the feeling of Beauty, with a capital *B.* I reflected on Beauty and the energy-sharing perceptions Redfield had written about. I remembered he had recommended focusing on the Beauty of a thing as a way to begin seeing its aura. I was not seeing any auras, but it occurred to me I was surely feeling them.

I was lying across Matthew's bed at the time, and after playing the keyboard for awhile, he came over and sat down next to me. We just sat in honey-golden silence for a few minutes. Then he kind of chuckled and quietly commented about feeling an intense energy in the air. I turned to him incredulously, "You feel it too?" I then went on to tell him about Redfield's book and the insights about energy-sharing I had just been pondering. That night marked a new level of collaborative rhythm exploration for us.

Once in a while, Matthew and I opened our circle and invited between three and five drumming friends to join us. We all began having similar experiences together. This energetic flow would simultaneously descend upon and come up through us and our drums, and it felt good. Damn good. Everyone remarked on it, though we didn't quite have the language yet to articulate our experiences to ourselves, never mind each other, and so we didn't. It was just a common understanding that we liked what we were doing, how it felt, and years later we're still doing it—regularly.

As Matthew and I continued to explore the ecstatic experience through drumming, not calling it that until much farther down the road, I noticed my journal entries seemed to be organizing themselves into a kind of mapping of the territory. This opened up more dialogue between Matthew and me. He too was beginning to have intense spiritual experiences through rhythm and was receiving information on the ecological structures of rhythm.

We talked more about what we were doing and how we got to that deep, inner place where this energy would come and play through us. We noted such things as our personal attitudes and type of rhythms that seemed conducive to initiate them; what it felt like on an emotional and physical level; how our perceptions shifted during the journey; things that happened along the way; and noting the various challenges of integrating ourselves and our experiences back into mundane reality.

Throughout this time I was slowly awakening to a growing recognition of rhythm and the ecstatic experience as a profound shamanic healing modality with very ancient roots. Rhythm was a gateway to altered states of consciousness, and more importantly, it was a path into the soul and deep worlds that lay within and beyond. The spirit of rhythm came and wooed me in all areas of my life, not only tantalizing me through the seductive polyrhythms of Africa and the Caribbean, but also in the wind rippling through the leaves of the towering maple outside the kitchen, in the swirling ecstatic flight of tiny winged bugs. Rhythm flirted with me like a lover, unfurling its beauty and captivating me with its rapture. I found it utterly irresistible. I had become a fool for the Pulse. I started seeing it, feeling it, breathing it everywhere. I was always in the embrace of rhythm. And this rhythm was alive! It beckoned me like a siren's call to journey with it deeper into other worlds. How could I possibly say no?

There was another shaman from the Circle who came to walk with me at this time. Much of what I have discovered through rhythm has been guided or impressed upon me through my relationship with him, the one I call Nadu.

Unlike the others, my meeting and perception of Nadu seemed to congeal slowly over time. As I took my first steps in learning some of the traditional African rhythms, I felt the presence of a new spirit around me while I drummed. The presence of this spirit grew stronger as I began to develop some fluency with the language of the drum, while patiently nursing myself through the occasional blister and bruised palm. The night I finally met Nadu, he virtually leapt out of the ethers before me. Matthew and I had one of our organic drumming sessions that night, and I felt inspired to retire early to my room, spurred by a compelling urge to write.

As I settled in and the words started bubbling around, I happened to glance up into a mirror sitting before me. I saw my face, but at first glance it appeared slightly fuzzy, as if there were a bit of a cloud around it. I blinked and it cleared. It was at that moment that my mind was flooded with his face, crystal clear before me. Since I work primarily clairsentiently, receiving such a vibrant clairvoyant image is somewhat unusual.

But there he was. A full round face of dark bluish-brown skin, so lustrous it virtually shone. His eyes, incredibly bright and sparkling beneath raised eyebrows, held a greeting. His face was framed with medium-length dreads that playfully spilled over his forehead and ears. That night he appeared with a stripe of blue that followed his jaw line across his chin from ear to ear. This blue stripe is sometimes dotted with yellow, as it was that night. The name that popped into my mind was Nadu. I once asked him if that was indeed his name. He just shook his head and smiled, waving my question off as if brushing away a pesky gnat, "It is close enough. It'll do."

Nadu is a bit shorter than I, I'd guess about five feet, five inches, with a wiry, energetic body. When I first met him, he felt to hail from or have a strong affinity for both the African and Aboriginal cultures. More recently though, I've had a stronger sense that he's African, but frequently travels with an Aboriginal companion. There is some strong affinity between the two of them, as if they are like twin stars drawn together in a singular solar orbit of spiritual purpose.

From my perspective, the sheer vibrancy of Nadu's energy somewhat eclipses the presence of his Aboriginal companion, if this second spirit does indeed exist. It has also occurred to me that what I currently perceive as an eclipse may actually be more indicative of a future relationship quietly gestating in the background, for I've had the intuition I may come to work with this other person at a later time; the bridge between the two of us being Nadu. The thoughts Nadu brought to me that first night are contained in the Initiation Prayer at the beginning of chapter 4.

About a month later, in March 1994, three months after Matthew and I had begun our weekly drumming journeys, we attended Drum and Dance Saturday, an event sponsored by Earth Drum Council, held every other Saturday night in Harvard Square. It was to be a special evening because Onye Onyemaechi was back in Boston.

Although the event's roots could be traced back to people who gathered to drum before and after outdoor concerts on the Cambridge Common in the late seventies, it was largely Onye who organized and solidified the current incarnation of Drum and Dance in the early eighties, before he moved to California a few years later. After Onye moved away, Drum and Dance passed through a few good hands to be inherited in 1990 by Jimi and

Morwen Two Feathers, the cofounders of Earth Drum Council where it resides today. It is believed that Drum and Dance Saturday in Harvard Square may very well be the oldest continuous drum circle of its kind in the United States.

An interesting point of synchronicity is that I had met Onye years ago. For a while he attended the First Spiritual Temple where I was studying and practicing as a medium. I came to be acquainted with him at the Sunday services we attended. I remember him mentioning drumming back then, but I suppose I was not quite ripe for it at the time, so I never checked it out when the opportunity first presented itself.

So Onye was back in town this night. Jimi and Morwen were excited, and now that I was bonded to the Beat, I was also excited to meet Onye again. As I readied myself for the evening, I felt a growing anxiety. I was not particularly nervous about seeing Onye or drumming that night, but I felt edgy and jumpy for some reason. The same kind of edginess I often feel before a potent communication from spirit, although I didn't make that connection until later on in the evening.

Seeing Onye was great. We spoke for a few minutes, both of us remembering our meeting at the First Spiritual Temple years before and mutual friends we knew from there. Then we settled in to drum. I was still feeling very edgy, but I was handling it. The drumming helped move it through me. Someone called the break for Kakilambe, a West African song traditionally associated with the harvest time. I was seated, playing jembe next to Onye, who was playing *jun-jun* with my friend Rodger on *gun-gon*, which are both bass drums. The two of them hooked up in an amazing bass rhythm, in drum speak referred to as "the bottom." I began to ease back into the rhythm, playing the basic part I knew, feeling it sync up with the bottom.

I then became aware of a very excited Nadu nearby. I could feel his energy hovering close to me. My skin began to prickle. I felt the space inside my chest expand and tingle. My head became light. Soon I heard voices rise up in chanting above the drumming. I looked around to see who was singing. No one was. Yet there it was plain as day, the overtone chanting of many voices swirling through the rhythms.

The presence of Nadu grew stronger; his energy began blending with my own. He asked me, "May I speak?" and I knew he was asking if he could drum. I responded "Yes," and in an instant, he was there in my body with me. This was not at all uncomfortable or frightening, as it was very similar to many of my clairsentient experiences of spirit communication. I often feel myself energetically merging with a spirit communicator and I had come to know Nadu over the past several months and trusted him a great deal. Although I had many experiences of clairsentient mergings with spirit, I had never experienced a spirit communicator animating my body in this way.

My hands had now become his. I watched, totally amazed, as they drummed rhythms I'd never heard or done myself. This is not to say I transformed into a virtuoso that night, but I was definitely drumming at a level distinctly beyond my usual capabilities. My spirit was filled and lifted with an ecstatic energy almost indescribable. I was no longer in a church in Harvard Square . . . I went somewhere else. Wherever I went was similar to the journeys Matthew and I had begun over those past few months, but this was potently cranked up another several notches. I don't know how long we played Kakilambe, but I heard afterward it was about forty-five minutes.

Nadu played through me for a period of time, I'm not sure how long, perhaps not more than five minutes, but it felt like it was much longer. When he was done, he returned my hands and thanked me. I settled back into a basic Kakilambe part, every once in a while throwing in a couple of riffs I had just picked up from Nadu. I was blown away by what had happened and very content to just stretch out and revel in the hot groove that now filled the room.

When the song came to a close, I couldn't speak. I looked over at Onye with a grin on my face.

He looked back at me sheepishly and said, "I hope it was okay I played so long, but the Grandfathers! The Grandfathers spoke to me through the drum. They kept telling me to 'Keep playing! Keep playing!'" I assured Onye that, as far as I was concerned, the song was absolutely perfect. I didn't mention my experience with Nadu. Although Nadu didn't drum through me anymore that night, I felt him lingering nearby for the rest of the evening.

As Matthew and I attended Drum and Dance Saturday we began stepping outside right after "middle circle." Middle circle is the halfway point of the evening where the drumming stops for a few minutes and everyone gathers together in a circle to share their name and any announcements of interest to the community. Because Matthew and I had been playing together at home and visiting with ecstatic energy through the drum there, we took the opportunity to step outside after middle circle and hold a short intention circle inviting that energy to join us here— the same way we began our drumming journeys at home.

One night, on our way back into Drum and Dance proper, Matthew ventured a question. "I'm almost afraid to say this because it may sound really egocentric, but I've been noticing what seems to be a connection between our intention circle and how the rhythms and energy seem to sync up right after we come back in. Have you noticed it, or is it just me?" It was as if Matthew gave words to something submerged just below the surface of my awareness. I hadn't really noticed it before, but when he spoke this, a piece of the puzzle was unearthed from somewhere in my psyche. I had intuited a correlation and now we both began to watch for it.

We started meeting with a few other friends for intention circles after Drum and Dance's middle circle. As we did, we noticed that many times while we were in the circle outside stating our intentions inviting this healing, ecstatic energy to join us, we actually could hear the rhythms shifting, opening, and syncing up. In my years of working as a medium with absent healing I had come to see the power of prayer and some of the ways it seemed to have a positive affect in people's lives. But this was a bit different. From our rudimentary experiments, it seemed as if we were observing the effects our prayers had on the energy of the rhythms moving through the people drumming and dancing on the other side of the wall, and the effects were sometimes near instantaneous. There was no mistake about it, the energy was increasingly more ecstatic.

Collectively, Matthew and I and others have run this "experiment" at least a couple of hundred times, with similar results. I'd estimate that in approximately ninety percent of the cases, ecstatic energy and rhythms begin to manifest fairly immediately, either during or within ten minutes after completing the intention circle.

Years later, I attended a workshop given by Bradford Keeney on healing and ecstasy, and he made a comment as we prepared to enter a community healing experience. "All it takes is one sincere prayer to bring this energy." Through my observations and experiences I know without a doubt this is true. The implications this one simple experiment has for the power of focused thoughts and feelings in influencing energy and cocreating reality is staggering.

Nadu continued to visit during the drumming journeys at home, giving me shards of information or commentary about working with rhythm in a healing way. I was practicing alone one day and I entered a very repetitive rhythm on the jembe. It was entrancing and relaxing, but I had the thought that perhaps I was limiting myself and wondered if I should spend some time breaking out of this rhythm my body had attuned itself to. Or was there some greater value to what I was doing? Nadu interrupted my thoughts. He encouraged me to change just one thing in the rhythm every few cycles. Where I had played a downbeat in the rhythm for a few cycles, improvise by leaving it out the next time for another few cycles, and keep improvising the rhythm ever so slightly. Don't think, just let go. Let it happen.

I did this and noticed I would eventually come back around to the original rhythm. In doing so, it created a kind of spiral effect through the rhythms. As this spiral moved through the song, I had the clear sense that it reflected a story being told through the rhythms. Nadu confirmed this. If asked, I couldn't render the story in verbal language, but I was aware of it imparting knowledge. Nadu kept encouraging me toward this type of playing, stressing that it was an important aspect to learn, or more accurately, it was an important aspect of rhythm to let go into.

In June of that year, Matthew, Brad, a friend of his visiting from out of town, and I went to Drum and Dance Saturday. When we arrived at the church, Jimi was there to greet us with some unexpected news. The space had been mistakenly double-booked that night and it turned out that Drum and Dance was without a location. We put our heads together and came up with an idea. Since it was a balmy spring evening, why not meet down by the river and have Drum and Dance outside? We picked a location and as people continued to arrive we spread the word. I wrote up a note with directions and tacked it on the door. People loaded drums and percussion instruments into their vehicles and headed over to the stone circle behind the public theater on the Charles River.

We arrived and were without light except for a lone candle and a flashlight that was lowered into the stone pit in the center of the circle. The glow emanating forth provided enough light to navigate around the circle, while creating an ambiance well suited for altered states of consciousness. We settled in, surrounded by a grove of trees, and the drumming began slowly.

After a half hour or so the rhythms and energy were not coming together. Things were disjointed. Matthew and I decided to step away and invite Brad to join us for an intention circle. As we sometimes do, we brought out a pipe and some marijuana, something we considered a sacrament. We found that one or two hits helped in parting the veils, sensitizing us to the deeper patterns and dialogues occurring within the rhythms. To smoke more than this was not necessary. As Matthew placed a pinch in the bowl and offered it to Brad, we began voicing our intentions, one at a time. Matthew then turned and offered the pipe to me. I took a deep hit and silently reiterated my prayer to spirit. Then Matthew reloaded the pipe for himself.

During this time the disjointed, cacophonous rhythms of the drum circle continued nearby. But as the smoke melted into my being and I held my intention in mind, they began to shift. In less than two minutes they had transformed into a greater order, an undulating serpent, waking up, breathing fire. I heard a song within the song, strong and clear, and it told me to get myself back to the circle, quickly. The message came from Nadu. I excused myself to Matthew and Brad saying I had to return to the circle *now*, and literally ran across the field. I didn't wait for the second hit.

My jembe was there waiting for me. I found my place on the stone wall and started playing the song Nadu had called me with. The song he was still singing. His energy became more electrified. I felt him drawing closer to me, so close his aura came to penetrate, to overshadow my own and mingle with me. Nadu didn't have to ask this time. Through our energetic connection I sensed he wanted to speak through the drum again. I offered him my hands and he eagerly accepted.

Like the night Onye had been in town a few months earlier, Nadu again merged with me and played through my hands, this time for a long time. But what he did when he first joined with me was to spend some time instructing me about rhythm. My attention focused and he led me to isolate and discern specific rhythms being played by different drums around me. In an organic drum jam of many different drums and levels of experience, this is often a difficult feat to accomplish. I couldn't tell if I was accomplishing this feat of attention purely of my own accord or if somehow the merging of Nadu heightened my ability to do this. In other words, was I perceiving this strictly through my own senses or through the joining of Nadu's and my own?

In any event, Nadu started playing different songs through my drum to each of the drum rhythms around the circle, one at a time. In many ways, he was demonstrating what he had been telling me about at home—the creation of rhythmical spirals. As he shifted into each new song within the overall song being played, my attention would be drawn to the particular drum he was playing with. I began to track his movement through the circle in this way, which I realized is what he wanted me to do.

I've noticed that many of the teachings that came through Nadu and other shamans from the Circle of Shaman were given in a similar way. They came, not so much with specific direction, but by laying out clues and patterns and pieces of the puzzle that were up to me to put together. I've realized the many benefits of this approach. One is that it enabled me to become more fluent and self-sufficient in operating in the realm of the mythic and symbolic. Nadu was providing a perfect demonstration of that this night.

He spent probably ten or fifteen minutes showing me the various songs he was singing to each of the different drums around the circle. (I had my eyes closed through much of this so was not following it visually.) Then he initiated something new. Before he did, he told me there was a message he had to deliver to the people. He then ceased the individual song-singing he had been doing. I now became aware once more of the collective song rising from the circle. To this, Nadu began drumming a rhythm that seemed to weave together the others in a complex polyrhythm. As he did this, the level of ecstatic energy rose dramatically in the circle. I could hear all the other drums responding, spiraling their rhythms around this greater song. I opened my eyes and people were dancing fervently with the Pulse, with the undulating fire-breathing serpent, as if almost lifted off the ground by a rapture that filled the air and the bodies. It was almost as if the energy were quaking underground beneath our feet.

This rhythmical rapture continued moving through the circle building in intensity, and when the song came to a close a little while later, people whooped and clapped. Drum rolls sounded. Bells rang out. The circle had experienced something incredible together: ecstasy. And people united their voices together in celebratory recognition. As the song drew to a close, the intimate energy link Nadu and I shared separated and reorganized itself back into its individual strands. I loosened the straps of the jembe, stretched my arms out in front of me and put my cheek down against the drum skin, letting out a deep breath and slowly letting in the awareness of what had just happened. Arana, my other housemate, who had been playing jun-jun, came over, his face beaming, and kidded me, "Hey, don't stop now." But I felt I just wanted to put my drum back in its case for the evening.

The ecstatic energy continued and another rhythm started up. People were playful, animated, creative. I pulled my drum close and tried to play again, but it was a half-hearted attempt. After a few minutes I realized the best I could do was to mimic some of the rhythms Nadu had just played. I could do that, but it wasn't very appealing. I checked in with myself and got clear that my only real desire at that moment was to put the drum away and just bask in the energy for a while, which is what I did. I reveled in the ecstatic energy observing it move through the drummers and dancers for the rest of the night. Nadu, also satisfied and contented, had some commentary.

He explained to me something I was beginning to discover through our work together: that rhythm is an energetic frequency that is and can be infused with information. Rhythm is a language used to communicate between the worlds. It doesn't matter that such communication bypasses the verbal mind, for it carries its own higher rationality which speaks directly with the DNA of the body and the energy fields flowing through, emanating from, and surrounding it, in what is sometimes referred to as the aura or auric egg.

Nadu also said that such a communal experience of ecstasy indicates a strong, clear connection—a bridge has been made between the ordinary and nonordinary worlds. The message contained in the rhythms is transmitted along this ecstatic frequency. He added that when ecstasy continues long after the original song that delivers it to the people, it is a very good sign that healing occurred for all who gathered to share this sacred space, through this connection between the worlds.

Less than a year later Matthew moved to North Carolina, and a thousand miles apart we continued our work exploring and mapping this experience we were now calling ecstasy. He, through articulating the more technical rhythmic perspective, me through the more spiritual-emotional experience. Yet it was starkly obvious to us that we were petals of the same flower. Our conversations always had the effect of cross-pollinating and enriching each other's focus in this area.

Around the time Matthew moved away, I became involved in a women's magical group that was just forming, initiated by Lori, a friend I had come to know through the drum and dance community. In some ways it represented a feminine enclave whose members bridged two mature, artistic, progressive communities in the Boston area—Dance New England (DNE) and Earth Drum Council (EDC). Morwen Two Feathers was one of these women. Our relationship solidified as we worked together planning and staffing EDC events.

She and I discovered we had similar interests and visions in working with drumming, dancing, and rhythm in a healing and transformational way. We began meeting on a regular basis to brainstorm other workshops, proposals, and writing projects. It didn't take us long to begin dancing immediately following the business portion of our meetings. In the process, we noticed that some profound insights often emerged through the dance, as if the dance opened our visionary centers wider.

Not long after, the women's magical group began to incorporate evocative recorded music and free-form dance as an integral part in some of our rituals. We danced as goddesses, we danced as elements, we danced as our shadow selves, we danced as our spirit allies. We danced to the Earth. We danced to the stars. We danced to each other. We danced to heal, to pray, to celebrate, to stretch into places we'd never been before. All with results that infused our inner worlds with a vibrancy I had never known before, and yet, it also felt very familiar. Through the dance, but particularly through the caring, honest, authentic space we've created as our foundation, the filaments of our circle have been woven into a vibrant tapestry, a magic carpet we continue to ride together into other worlds.

9 Elements of the Ecstatic Realm

Ecstasy is the higher self in action.

Chris Griscom

At the heart of the unconscious is what many experience as the source of life itself, and which some call God. . . . Such union is the culmination of all seeking, all desire; it is the most cherished of all experiences of which man is capable.

Stolaroff

Myth is not fully understood unless one enters into an altered state of consciousness; yet the myth itself. . . may provide the trigger or catapult for ecstatic experience.

Stephen Larsen

IT TOOK SEVERAL YEARS FOR ME to see that the consistent thread weaving through everything the Circle of Shaman had to share centered around the shamanic flight of ecstasy. I've realized that the healing and authentic power we seek, that which is necessary for our survival and collective well-being, emanates from the heart of this experience. How we cultivate ecstasy, distill the wisdom found within it, and bring the results into all our relations, will largely determine our success in midwifing the deepened citizenry required of us in these times. I was prompted to research a sampling of literature on the subject of ecstasy from a variety of perspectives, including psychotropic journeys and mystical awakenings. I've interwoven these with my own observations.

The early misconception I had, and one that is prevalent in our culture, was believing that ecstasy was simply an experience of unbounded joy. It certainly can be this and often is. However, (a large caveat here) it's important to note that joy is just one aspect of this multidimensional, holohedral experience.

"Ecstasy is a complex emotion containing elements of joy, fear, terror, triumph, surrender and empathy."[1] The word is taken from the Greek *ekstasis,* meaning "displacement, trance, to take flight, to drive out of one's senses." This feeling of displacement is where we derive the saying, "I was beside myself . . ." You suddenly feel displaced, outside yourself or your ordinary experience of reality. The *Women's Encyclopedia of Myths and Secrets* defines it well as "standing forth naked." Einstein referred to ecstasy as the "ultimate religious feeling state." Other modern terms for it are "peak experience" or "cosmic consciousness." Shamanic ecstasy can be described as a union and communion with the sacred realm that permits the shaman to perform her work.

The feeling that pervades the ecstatic experience is one of being connected with something greater than yourself—God, Goddess, the Tao, the Great Spirit, the Sacred Realm, the Pulse, whatever name you call it.

Nothing is hidden in this place. There are no secrets. Any masks or personas the profane self holds up to mitigate reality are lost on the ecstatic experience. They are temporarily dissolved, cast or blown aside, hence this indelible feeling of standing forth naked. It is a place of utter vulnerability because this degree of self-revelation and spontaneous disclosure of the nature of psyche and reality is far beyond our ordinary experience of ourselves and the mundane world we inhabit.

Most of us live in a daily reality in which we habitually armor ourselves physically, emotionally, mentally, or spiritually. While there are situations that warrant such armoring, this defensive process causes alienation from the Soul. If this is a chronic condition, it cuts us off from the source of our being while our lives are slowly drained of meaning. The shaman seeks to restore this connection through the ecstatic experience. According to Eliade, "Shamanic cure involves ecstasy because illness is regarded as an alienation of the soul."[2]

In ecstasy you come to meet something much greater than yourself, and also something of which you know you are part. You are encompassed by a presence alive and informed. A presence that looks back at you, while at the same time looks out from within you: a storytelling presence that dances with you, sings through you, and infuses you with insights, both arcane and obvious. This presence may be experienced as a being, a cosmic community, both, or something else entirely. As Redfield discovers in *The Celestine Prophecy*[3]

> I perceived everything to be somehow part of me. As I sat on the peak of the mountain looking out at the landscape falling away

from me in all directions, it felt exactly as if what I had always known as my physical body was only the head of a much larger body consisting of everything else I could see. I experienced the entire universe looking out on itself through my eyes.

Through this kind of meeting you realize an unequivocal truth in what the shamans say: "Everything that is, is alive!" All of creation is alive! Everything that exists is ultimately sentient, permeated with consciousness. (Or perhaps it is more accurate to say that consciousness is permeated with form.) This realization enables new forms of communication and relationship, not only with one's deeper self, but with other species and worlds as well. The shaman initiate is one who learns how to enter into this greater realm of relationship and communication.

In the ecstatic experience you may feel yourself standing in a circle of creation with all that is, where everyone and everything is equal. Here it is revealed that the fundamental nature of this circle is egalitarian, and this equal regard for all is the underpinning of reality. No one thing is favored more than another. Your life is no more or less significant than that of the frog sleeping on the lily pad, or the logger felling another acre of rain forest, or the shooting star blazing across the sky, drawn down from its celestial journey.

Ecstasy is both a wide-angle lens across the furrowed landscape of reality and a mirror reflecting the image of who and what you are. With unfettered frankness and without judgment it exposes the limitations and hubris of any ego or anthropocentric dogma held by the profane self. With the same passion and clarity, it reveals the dharma and gifts of who and what you are that you either tend not to see or hesitate to accept. Ecstasy holds forth that we are fields of flowers whose roots stretch deeply into the dark, rich soil of the One Heart, blooming forth its many faces of power, humor, wisdom, compassion, and creativity.

I occasionally use psychotropic sacraments in my ecstatic journeys. In one such experience I was walking through the woods

late at night, bathed in reverie and the soft light of a first quarter
moon. I came upon a clearing where a multitude of dead trees
stretched their lifeless limbs in frightful gestures toward the sky,
as if the moment of death froze them in a posture of frustration
and despair. They appeared to be vehemently cursing their trans-
gressors as life took leave of them. And there was this feeling that
the humanity I carried in my being was the object of this curse. A
wave of discomfort and intimidation overtook my previous inspired mood.

While I was debating whether to slink away or to remain
with the trees, feeling uncomfortable, an inner voice cut through
the din, paraphrasing something Joseph Campbell had written:

> Our demons are our own limitations, which shut us off from the
> realization of the ubiquity of the spirit. And as each of these
> demons is conquered in a vision quest, the consciousness of the
> quester is enlarged, and more of the world is encompassed . . .
> a devil is a god who has not been recognized.[4]

I looked at this meeting with the trees as though I had come
face to face with a god wearing the face of a demon. What did it
have to teach me? I wondered. And so I stood there in silent
contemplation with the dead trees screaming toward heaven. What
I began to notice was a kind of vibrant elegance in these trees and
their dance of death. I honored them as artisans of this beauty. As
I did, my fear and discomfort melted away. I felt gratitude that
my journey had brought me to the underworld, to the feet of
these great beings and even to the discomfort I had felt.

The trees responded, their demonic garb now discarded. Their
circle opened to me and I was invited in. I felt acknowledged as
kin and regarded with equal respect. But it's not as if this invitation and kinship were not there a moment before. The invitation
came when I realized our deeper kinship within myself. I gra-
ciously accepted this joint acknowledgment and stepped into the

circle, our circle, acutely aware that I was no more or less important in the grand scheme of things than the naked sentinels at this portal to the underworld.

The tree gods, led by the most frightful-looking one, then filled me with a quiet strength and fortitude, qualities carried in their lives and still carried in the underworld. They helped me take in and ground this gnosis-of-the-moment in my being. The Most Frightful One explained that the chilling gestures were not a curse on humans, but rather a loud visual display from this tree tribe observing the mindlessness that begets disease. Their chilling gestures are meant to help wake a sentient being from its slumber and the nightmare of self-imposed alienation from creation, whatever world it resides in.

"Humans have no monopoly on ignorance," the Most Frightful One added.

It is this experience of oneness and fundamental kinship with creation that is the primary archetypal footprint of the ecstatic experience. "The oneness of the ecstatic experience enables the initiate to see and experience from a divine viewpoint, and therefore to see and experience how the spirit world, the human world, and the nature world are wholly one in essence, although different in appearance."[5]

On another occasion, this unitive feeling similarly expressed itself through me in poetic form following an ecstatic dance:

No political embargo or priestly admonitions
can stop the mother ship.

She responds in her fullness
velvet-gloved lightning bolt torching fields
where the tangled ersatz grows
obliterating lines between good bad and ugly
gathering up all of who you are
in her deft ecstatic hands

joyful
trembling
A dark pregnant pleasure then fills too bright
and overflows!

Ecstasy is the felt experience of dialogue with the ground of
your being, with the circle of creation—a dialogue that is always
going on in the deeper soundings of the Soul. Ecstasy comes and
assists the shamanic archetype to restore the connection and bring
the awareness of this dialogue to the profane self.

This dialogue may incorporate words, but also goes well beyond them and the mechanics of conversation we're so familiar
with. A synthesis of images, kinesthetic impressions, emotional
stimuli, and clairsentient insights comprise the language and currency of ecstasy. The experience itself takes place in a realm that
extends far beyond, yet incorporates, the three-dimensional world
we know. This other realm, the imaginal or mythic realm, the sacred world of the shaman, is an expanded interior world that our
common everyday language is not well suited to circumscribe, partly
because the creation of verbal and written communication is primarily a linear process designed to negotiate three-dimensional reality. So a strictly rational approach to ecstasy is rarely successful.

The fullness or contents of one's experience with ecstasy are
often ineffable. Although words may not capture the fullness of
the experience for others, the poetic use of metaphor and imagery
can well relate the inherent profundity, the deep transformational
potential that ecstasy bears. A potential swelling to burst from the
bud, representing a new self begging to be born in profane reality.

We can discern both this ineffable quality and unitive nature as
Black Elk relates his visionary ecstatic experience as a young boy to
John Neihardt in *Black Elk Speaks*:[6] "While I stood there, I saw
more than I can tell, and I understood more than I saw; for I was
seeing in a sacred manner the shapes of all things in the spirit, and
the shape of all shapes as they must live together like one being."

Like a dream, the language of the ecstatic experience is often filled with an incredible array of profound and prolific nuances, sometimes subtle, sometimes blatant. Every image, every sensation is laden with information that floods the senses and conscious mind, at times spilling over into other sense perceptions. Colors may be heard or tasted; music and sounds may be seen. This multiperceptual phenomenon is known as synesthesia, or cross-sensing. It is fairly common in the ecstatic experience.

This is not surprising, for the natural proclivity of ecstasy is to invigorate and enliven the metaphorical mind. What the metaphorical mind essentially does is perceive connections and associations between things "dissimilar," to see the relationship and common thread that weaves together what may appear on one level as diverse and disparate elements. This is one of the reasons why poetry and inspired prose move us so. Metaphor is the language of the Soul aware and experiencing its divine connection in the world and its intimate relationship with the diversity of creation—an embodied soul in the process of re-cognizing, re-knowing itself through its relationships.

In this way, ecopsychology is also a natural extension of the metaphorical mind. For it is an understanding that one's intimate connection with the environment, a connection filled with eros and compassion, is necessary for a healthy life for body and soul. Synesthesia is another expression of the metaphorical mind in action, another avenue of sensual poetics that brings awareness of this unitive reality to the profane self. Consider this account of an ecstatic experience by Rowena Pattee in *Shaman's Path*.[7]

> I felt my boundaries beyond dimensions break into pure ground. My body was fanning out into a limitless universe. As I drifted up will-lessly, impalpable, translucent, unearthly colors shimmered within my vast body. The whole extent of my awesome body now focused to a central point at the core of the earth,

celestial vermilions, magentas, indigos, ceruleans, viridians creating an ecstatic song beyond sensation. The "sound" of color
rose like ambrosia up through subterranean channels into conti-
nents and nations throughout the earth. I experienced the sound
of colors of my soul permeate the mountains and valleys of China,
the rivers and deserts of Egypt, and the vast steppes of Russia.
My body was the bone of the earth, flesh of the creatures, blood
of the seas, breath of the skies. I saw the colors of myself as the
soul of China, Greece, Europe, Africa, India, Australia, the Oce-
anic Islands, and the Americas. The shimmering shades of colors
moved in great chants beyond the surface of the whole earth and
out into the firmaments and beyond.

References to rhythm and music abound in ecstatic literature
because they represent the aboriginal language and dialogue dynamics of this realm. In the ecstatic experience, many different
"voices" may be heard speaking together simultaneously, yet the
dialogue is frequently coherent and harmonious. It is often heard
as chanting, a song, or a rhythm of some sort in which the whole
can be comprehended while the distinct voices within it are also
acknowledged. As Pattee points out, you are " . . . simultaneously
aware of a limited vantage where the identities are separate and an
ecstatic, divine vantage where the separate identities are, in essence,
identical."[8] In the ecstatic experience, these separate identities are
integrated, knitted together in such a way as to comprise a singular
identity or voice, yet there is no compromise of identity integrity
of the individuals. The knitting itself, this silk in the web that weaves
it all together also has a voice unfolding into the ecstatic symphony
where one unquestionably experiences the whole as being much
greater than the sum of the parts.

In the profane world it is cacophonous and disorienting—
and next to impossible for me to listen and to comprehend more
than one person speaking at a time. But when I move to a divine
or shamanic vantage, I also invoke noetic abilities native to that

realm. These abilities allow comprehension of ecstatic dialogue composed of many different voices speaking simultaneously, organizing themselves in a particular rhythm or song in which the fullness of the message can be comprehended by the psyche. The Circle of Shaman indicates that this is why music has such a powerful, timeless, and universal appeal. It exemplifies the dynamics of communication in the sacred realm, a dynamic that our essential selves are all familiar with.

There have been many occasions at drumming circles when someone will remark incredulously, "Did you hear that chanting? I looked around to see where it was coming from and I could see no one singing. Yet I heard it as clear as day." When I hear such chanting, it's another signal to me that the sacred gateway has been opened and ecstasy is flowing forth into the space from the other side.

Ecstasy infuses you with a knowing and wisdom that feels to exude not only from your connection with the surrounding environment, but also from every cell within the body itself.

> One senses the aware presence of spirit infusing the structures of the body and the images and attitudes of the mind. Awareness expands to include all parts of the body, all aspects of the mind, and the "higher reaches" of Spirit—thus permitting a kind of re-connecting, a re-membering of the totality of our experience, an access to forgotten truths.[9]

This knowledge is carried subliminally until it's released into awareness from deep within the body's substrata of DNA and star stuff; it goes well beyond what the ego or the profane self has culled through its accumulation of experiences in this lifetime.

Ecstasy is the bridge that connects the profane world with this transcendent reality—the shamanic sacred world. It is the doorway that leads to worlds within worlds which we are and of which we are a part. With unabashed poignancy and paradox, it centers the heart in the shimmering web of all our relations. It is the axis mundi, the world tree of the psychic landscape, the center of the psychic solar system from which all things emanate, spiral out, and return again, the alpha and the omega. The ecstatic experience reveals us to be very large beings stretching across the cosmos—living, breathing, evolving temples of *akashic* records whose cosmic information is immanently available to us and evocable through the kivas of our own bodies.

10 Opening to Ecstasy

Rhythm touches deep chords of resonance in our ancestral memories; whenever we connect with other human beings through rhythmic music, dance, or drumming, the memory of humankind as one family arises.

Reinhard Flatischler

Through the great and small rhythms of consciousness—through cycles as small as the moment or as large as civilization itself— we step forward, not just as parts in creation, but as creators in creation.

Charles Johnston

We humans are a vast system of systems and subsystems; to make conscious use of the complex wisdom of the body is to achieve a sublime orchestral experience of the self and its many ecologies.

Jean Houston

The body does not lie.

Martha Graham

ACCORDING TO NADU, rhythmical empathy represents the core shamanism. He indicates that all shamanic techniques are essentially a conscious and specialized working with rhythmic patterns of the cosmos. The shaman learns how to read and engage what is contained within the great cosmic flow in order to effect change. The shaman, in one form or another, "dances" with energies of the cosmos that organize and present themselves in various mythic forms, such as animal powers, spirit guides, devas, daimons, elementals, archetypes, and angels.

Rhythm lies at the heart of ecstasy, for what is life but one grand polyrhythm? What is ecstasy but an experience of rhythmical entrainment, an empathic connection with your deeper self and something greater? While there are many pathways into the ecstatic experience, rhythm, at one level or another, plays an important role in all of them.

If you are new to this avenue of healing, how do you go about creating solid pathways into the experience of ecstasy and ecstatic healing using rhythm? How do you bring this experience into other areas of your life?

You can begin by developing rhythmical empathy, a conscious awareness that your life is already based in a rhythmical empathy with the cosmos. The exercises that follow are designed to simply bring an awareness of these rhythmical dances and a deeper sensitivity of their presence more to the fore of your mind. None of the following are exotic techniques. You need not purchase any special tools. You have everything you need right there in your body, your mind, and your heart. Although an able body is required to do some of the exercises, there are those you can do even if you do not have complete freedom of movement.

As you work with the following exercises, you may be surprised to feel like you've discovered something profound, and paradoxically, nothing really new. Just something you'd forgotten, perhaps, or was out of focus. As people enter the world of rhythm more consciously they usually exclaim, "Oh! I know this experience! I've been here before, I just never realized what it was." As you begin to immerse yourself in the rhythmic nature of the cosmos you may feel a distinct sense of familiarity. What people tend to discover is simply a greater context in which to experience rhythm, along with its profound capacity to facilitate healing, learning, and creativity.

The following are simple exercises designed to introduce the basics and from there rhythmical empathy tends to evolve very naturally. But first, if you happen to be one of those people who think you have no sense of rhythm, hold on! Indulge me if you will and close your eyes for a moment and feel the rhythm of your breath as it fills you, then empties. Find your pulse. Give it a soft audible sound as you feel it beat beneath your skin. That's rhythm. You carry it around in you all the time. It synchronizes itself with your breath and physical activity. An old African saying reminds us that if you have a heartbeat you can drum!

You can also easily grasp the flow of rhythm in walking, lovemaking, in the surf as it ebbs and flows against the beach, in the cycles of the moon and of the seasons, in the song of a bird, in the spinning of the Milky Way galaxy and of electrons in their subatomic spheres. As above, so below. Everywhere rhythm is happening.

To connect with the power of rhythm means to expand awareness.[1]

The exercises and suggested approaches in the next section will work with the breath, the voice, walking, music-making, and ecstatic dance to explore rhythm and heighten your awareness to its presence and flow within and around you. These techniques are based upon my own discoveries, coupled with results in the women's group, drumming circles, guidance from the Circle of Shaman, and research into other good work being done by growing numbers of people. The first portal into this world is the breath.

THE RHYTHM OF BREATH: GATEWAY TO THE SOUL

Through the rhythms of breathing, we engage the energy of life in a most intimate, visible, and felt way. The power of this particular body rhythm for ecstatic healing and awakening is easily overlooked. In our culture, it's easy to believe that it should be more complicated than just breathing, but it's not. Many people experience deep ecstasies and healing from the practice of breathing, in and of itself. An entire healing modality is devoted to the powers of the breath cycle, through much of the pioneering work of Stan Grof into transpersonal experiences. He developed a method called Holotropic Breathwork, based on his research into LSD experiences. There is another related field referred to as Rebirthing that also centers around breathing exercises.

Many meditative techniques as well, particularly from the Buddhist tradition, are structured around a focus on the rhythm of the inhale and exhale of the breath cycle. Working with the breath, you are able to shift brain wave patterns from the beta to the alpha state, which creates a meditative state of consciousness allowing for greater levels of healing and creativity.

The elements of this first exercise will be similar to those found in both meditation and forms of Breathwork and requires no other physical movement than breathing.

Allow yourself some quiet time on a regular basis, five minutes or less is a fine way to begin, to focus on this most primary rhythm happening in your body. No special preparations are needed. Sit quietly and comfortably and begin to feel the rhythm of your breath as it glides into your lungs, filling them, and then departs again. Feel how your chest gently rises and falls as it accomodates the air entering your body.

Observe how deeply the breath goes into you. After a few minutes, begin to guide it deeper into the bottom of your lungs, feeling your belly rise as it does so. At the end of your inhale, hold your breath and attention there for just a moment, a second, then allow yourself to exhale smoothly, holding again when you reach the place of empty breath before you inhale once more.

Becoming Fully Present
Breathe deeply in this way for a few cycles, return to shallower breathing for a few cycles, followed by deeper breathing again. Alternate back and forth between these two cycle levels. Allow the rhythm of your breathing to bring you into a clear presence with whatever reality is true for you at the moment. This is key in every exercise. Let your breath seek out and guide you to your inner truth, the gateway of your soul. Whatever that truth is, moment by moment, breathe with it. Feel the inner rhythm of this reality, of the different emotions within it, and how your breathing accomodates this reality, moves with it, flows through and around it. Let your breath dance with this inner reality. Give yourself the freedom to enjoy this breathing dance, even play with it, for it doesn't have to be overly serious.

If you find joy, breathe into it. Watch and feel with relaxed attention what occurs. If you find discomfort, see if you can meet it gently and breathe through it with ease. Let your thoughts slip away of their own. Simply enter into the felt experience of the rising and falling of your chest and your belly, the air passing in and out through the warm, moist passageways of your body, bringing this element of life inside yourself. You can do this anywhere: washing dishes, riding to work, preparing for an exam, waking up in the morning, and it can be done several times during the day if you wish, giving yourself a little respite and revitalization each time.

In his recent book, *Everyday Soul*,[2] Bradford Keeney offers many good exercises to expand your sense and expression of the rhythmic nature of life, within and without. In one exercise, a variation on the above, he encourages finding or creating an inner rhythm to accompany the rhythmic pulse of the breathing cycle. He advises us to

> proceed to fill the space in between [the inhale and exhale] with whatever improvised rhythms enter your imagination. Allowing the life situation you're in at the time of the exercise to shape the rhythm that is most fitting, whether it be a loud march or soft brush work on a finely tuned snare drum. . . . Concentrate so that your whole being is making rhythms that flow within the pulse of your breath.[3]

Another variation upon this breathing exercise is to play some favorite meditative or evocative music, whether it be soft and flowing or more percussive. As you listen to the music, use your breathe to draw the rhythms of the songs into your being. Breathe the rhythms deep inside yourself, allowing them to cleanse, heal, and enliven you. Choose a quality you wish to invigorate within yourself such as strength, joy, clarity, purpose, inspiration, compassion, or others of your choosing. You may wish to invigorate more than one in a breath session and this is fine. Bring each one to mind and create a vision or symbol of that quality, whatever comes through your imagination. For inspiration you may see yourself standing firmly on the Earth with arms outstretched toward heaven, a living connection between both these realms, watching as energy spirals from the cosmos into yourself where you transmute it into physical form; for example, a project that needs completion, or an issue that needs to be seen from a new perspective. When you are beginning, focus on the quality itself, not so on much the specifics of a desired outcome, to avoid having your awareness drawn out of your body and slipping back into heady, left-brain activity.

A symbol may embody and display a quality for you, such as a tree for strength, a flower for openness, or a mountain for groundedness. Images from tarot cards, or other inner-work cards may resonate with you. If you are not prone to being very imagistic you can just as well use a word as a mantra.

As you listen to the music, breathe the image or word into yourself, bringing your relaxed, attentive presence to it. Spend about ten to twenty minutes with this exercise. Close the exercise by allowing yourself a few minutes just to breathe for the sheer feeling and pleasure of doing it, and nothing else. Suggest to yourself that whenever you bring that image or vision to mind you will invigorate the quality it represents within yourself, each and every time.

If fears or discomfort arise at some points during any of these exercises, this is natural. The hectic pace of life can easily mask what's really true for us, what's going on inside and how we feel about it. Breathe into whatever comes up. If it is frustration or helplessness, breathe space around it. Be present with it. If tears begin to flow, make room for them. Let them happen. Stay in your body. Stay in your breathing. Constricting the flow of these feelings often creates deeper distress than the feelings themselves. Bringing them to your presence with breath and music helps in the process of moving and releasing them. Imagine your entire body being filled with the music and your breath cuddling all that is there within you.

Flowing with Inner Rhythms

As you become comfortable with this exercise, whether it is the first time you do it, or the thirtieth, you may find your body having a desire to sway along with the rhythm of the music and your breath. Encourage yourself to follow this rhythmic current as it exudes from a deeper place within, for you are entering into communion with your soul and the sacred realm of rhythms that reside there. See what movements the body wishes to make to support your healing vision work.

As your body sways and moves to the music and your breath, and you can be sitting or standing for this, you may also find that a chant or tone wants to weave itself into this rhythmic current moving through your body. If so, let this flow as well, whatever sound it may be. Allow your body to become an instrument for your breath, your voice, and these inner soul rhythms to play out through you. Through your breath, your movements, your chants and tones, you travel along the songlines of your soul deeper into the sacred realm. Let yourself explore the many dimensions of rhythm contained within your own body.

These exercises of attuning yourself to the rhythms of your breath can be taken outside into nature, and by all means, should be! A walking meditation through the woods, a park, along the ocean shore or a canyon trail, feeling the rhythm of the breath as it synchronizes itself with the rhythm of your walking, can be extremely relaxing, inspirational, and exhilarating.

Once you feel in touch with the synchronized rhythms of your breath and your walking, begin to expand your awareness out to embrace the rhythms of the natural environment embracing you in return, while maintaining the connection with your own rhythms. This may take a little practice. If you lose the connection with your own rhythms go back to the rhythm of your walking, then your breath. Then begin again to observe the various rhythms that are happening all around you. Perhaps there is a slight breeze causing the leaves to whisper or grasses to ripple in its wake, bringing slight temperature changes to brush across your skin. Breathe in these sounds and sensations. Don't let them stop at your ears or your eyes. Drink them deeply into yourself.

If you are walking along a river or near a pond, the sun may be sparkling like diamonds off the water as it flows by. Breathe in the rhythm of these sparkling diamonds, allowing their visual song to cleanse and vitalize you, or for no other reason than to simply enjoy and revel in the experience. At some point, exhale an appreciation or a prayer back into your environment as a way to express recognition and gratitude for the life-giving connection you're sharing together. Observe through your whole body, from the soles of your feet to the tips of your fingers to the top of your head, your back, your knees, and everything in between. Allow every inch of skin to absolutely revel in the great rhythmic sensations of the world humming within and all about you. In this very simple way you enter into a conscious dance with the cosmos itself.

There may be other people walking nearby, or clouds rambling overhead, or the song of a bird that comes and keeps you company on your rhythm meditation. Open yourself to embrace the expression of all these rhythms through your breath, through your walking, or just by sitting quietly, bringing them into yourself, exhaling beauty, breathing Soul in and back out into the world.

In *The Celestine Prophecy*, James Redfield recommends meditating on the beauty of a plant or other entity in nature. This is another wonderful entryway into the rhythms of Soul flowing through you and your environment, and an avenue to discover the diverse forms of nonhuman, yet sentient, ecstatic coconspirators all around you. If you have a favorite tree you visit, sit or lie underneath and do any of the variations of this exercise with it as your companion. Breathe in the beauty of your relationship together, offer full presence and acknowledgment in return through your exhale.

Welcome to the conspiracy—the "breathing together"—of ecstasy!

When we fill ourselves with soulful rhythms and play them out in the world, we breathe soul into others.[4]

GROUP RHYTHM MEDITATION

A few years ago, when I was living with my housemates Blake and Joe, we embarked together quite spontaneously on another variation of the above meditation. We lived across the street from a lovely pond that had several well-cared-for walkways encircling the perimeter. Since it was unusual that the three of us found ourselves together with free time, we took the opportunity to take a walk around the pond at dusk. It was either Blake or Joe who suggested we bring along small percussion instruments to play as we walked.

After picking up a pair of claves, a small bell, and whatever else it was that we brought with us that summer evening, we walked across the street to the pond and began a spontaneous, improvised rhythm on these instruments that entrained with our breathing and footsteps. Not only was it relaxing and joyful, but we could see it had a very definite influence upon those we passed.

I specifically remember two interesting and playful interactions. As we walked along, the sound and rhythm of our instruments gently enveloped and streamed out around like a large energetic bubble. The sounds echoed across the water reaching the ears of those a distance away from us.

An older couple, a gray-haired man and woman dressed in light sweaters to protect them from the evening chill approached us along the path from the opposite direction, arm in arm. As we came upon each other, the man's eyes lit up and he smiled seeing that the sounds he had heard were coming from us. Gently dropping the arm of his companion, he began to slowly and delicately twirl around upon the path before us! We moved around him in light footsteps of our own, the rhythms of our instruments synchronizing with his minstrel dance. Then he curtsied his appreciation to our nodding smiles, which returned the same, and he gracefully picked up the arm of his now giggling lady friend and they continued along their way.

Farther along we came upon a mother with three young children. As one, a little girl, ran out ahead, curious as to see what she had heard coming toward her along the wooded path, she suddenly stopped there agog when we came into view. With eyes and mouth wide open she exclaimed a moment later, "Mommy, mommy! What are they doing?"

"They're making music," the mother replied, as she glanced at us somewhat askance with a slight smile that was polite, but more ambivalent than the sparkling eyes of the elder couple we had just encountered.

I sensed that the little girl knew we were making music and was asking something more penetrating. She was at once delighted, yet in some obvious way almost taken aback by the sight and sounds of us. What was that powerful influence felt in the spontaneous, organic, rhythm walk of these three people?

So this is yet another variation of a rhythm meditation that you can do by yourself, or with others. If you are going to do it out in the general public, just be advised, as demonstrated by the above, that you will attract attention. If you wish to reduce this, bring along quieter percussion instruments, such as rattles, to create spontaneous rhythms while you walk or hike.

By consciously attuning yourself to the rhythms that move through your body, your interactions with others, and the environment, you'll find you're able to tap into increased levels of energy, creativity, and relaxation, essential cornerstones for healing and well-being.

These exercises will assist you in entering directly and concretely the rhythmic nature of life and Soul that flows through you and around you, everywhere. Set your imagination free to create other variations, and be sure to share them with others!

DRUMMING YOUR SOUL

Drumming is always an excellent way to increase your rhythmic sensitivity and receptivity. Over the past five years, drum circles have sprung up across the land and with them opportunities to experience the world of rhythm from various parts of the planet. You might look around your area to see if there are classes being offered. But you can also drum at home by yourself, through following your own intuition as I did, or through a curiousity just to explore and express yourself using the drum, as a way to give voice to what's true for you in the moment. For people who have discomfort speaking to others, drumming often acts as a good midwife between the inner voice and the world, to express what the voice may itself find intimidating.

There are several different types of small drums you can purchase for less than $100, from frame-style drums to the Middle Eastern *doumbeck*. But even a good plastic pail works, as well as other common items found in the kitchen. If you have a child, just watch or remember what he used to bang on, getting great glee out of the sound raised from striking object with implement, probably driving you crazy at the time. Drumming and rhythm-making is a natural instinct! There are also a growing number of good instructional videos and audiotapes that can introduce you to the wonderful world of global rhythms, both by playing and listening to them.

> We must have the beat, the heartbeat. We must know the pulse of life and experience it through dance, through music, to reaffirm our own rhythmic existence from the first drummer to ourselves.[5]

11 Trance Dance: Healing Through Ecstasy, Rhythm, and Myth

The first shamanic task is to free the body to experience the power of being.
Gabrielle Roth

Dancing and drumming are both powerful ways. . . to invoke energy. When combined, they create opportunities to be drawn into higher states of consciousness.
Ted Andrews

The basic wisdom already exists. It is there in the spiritual traditions of all cultures . . . . It is the truth we each know deep within. The question is how do we tap this wisdom? . . . Can it permeate our minds and hearts, enabling us to put this wisdom into practice? This is the real challenge facing us as we move into the next millenium.
Peter Russell

*P*leasingly plump ebony woman
likes her lace and lemonade,
feather in her hat on Sundays
A no-nonsense kind of gal
with medium-length hair
handsomely graying
artificially straightened
flipped up on the ends
Pours herself
into this yellow dress with white checks
sweat trickles down
an ample cleavage
where she tucks a fresh hanky.
She claps while I dance
and with delight
throws her head back
white teeth flashing, she exclaims
"Spirit will come move your body and heal it,
Praise the Lord!
Rhythm is our only Salvation!"

Message from a vivacious spirit woman
encountered in an ecstatic dance

My friend Tracy refers to herself as a disciple of the dance. She's a gifted performer and teacher of her adoration for rhythm, movement, and folkloric dance, and the time we spend together is typically punctuated by fits of ecstatic laughter on one hand and sublime journeys into the dance on the other. The anticipation alone as I drove out to see her one day began to entrain me with a special rhythm she and I share, a rhythm that often manifests visions and big dreams during our visit.

As I embarked on the two-hour trek out to her home in western Massachusetts, I played *Spirit Chaser* by Dead Can Dance on my tape deck and cranked up the volume. I began bobbing and swaying along in my car as I flowed toward Tracy. The words were haunting. "We are the birds of fire. We fly over the sky. Our light is a voice. We make a road for the spirit to pass over. . . . " I drank the words and the Pulse into myself as deeply as I could while still maintaining enough presence to drive.

Somewhere during this particular song, a vision began to unfold before my inner eyes, overlaying itself with the appearance of the road. During this time I was aware of both realities, the sacred and the mundane converging within me—one being attended to by my physical eyes, the other by my inner eyes.

What I saw in the inner landscape of this vision was a small circle of people sitting around a sacred fire in a darkened field. A shaman moved toward the fire and began to dance, mapping for the circle his journey into the sacred zone. The people began to sway to and fro, entraining themselves with the rhythm of his dance, feeling his dance inside themselves, joining him on his journey. Not long after, they were surprised to look around and notice they were no longer in the field where they began. They had attained such a strong rhythmical empathy with the shaman that they had actually been transported to the very place depicted by the shaman's dance.

Initially, my perspective in this vision was of a more distant view, from slightly above the field looking down on the circle. I could see the entire circle and from this vantage I could see that the group never left the field at all. I did not know the details of what they were seeing, but I knew that they had slipped through a portal, a doorway of some sort, into a nested reality. There they entered the shaman's landscape completely.

Then my perspective shifted and I was one of the participants sitting in the circle. I too opened up to the shaman's rhythms in my own body as he kept dancing, and now I could see the details of the environment in this other reality. I watched as, one by one, the people were drawn to different things in this new locale. I observed an oak tree "calling" to one man. He got up and approached the stately tree and stood gazing up into its branches. One woman was called by a large sprawling rock that she laid herself across in restful contemplation. A hawk lighted on a nearby branch, attracting the attention of another person. Each of these people turned their awareness now to that which had called them, and entered into communication with these companions. A voice from an unidentified source then spoke very clearly to me. "The shaman doesn't teach you anything. He or she brings you to a place in the sacred zone where the spirits then teach you."

Essentially this is the purpose of trance dance—to bring you to a place in the sacred zone where the spirits then teach you.

Shamans have codified their journeys through dance and song, chant and tale since ancient times. These are most likely the humble beginnings of ritual and theater, evolved from the shaman's artistic techniques to invite and include the tribe along on her journeys. The shaman understands the power of entrainment, of rhythmical empathy in its many forms and how it can be used to facilitate healing for the individual as well as the community. When people are united around a common vision and intention, it gathers energy, coalesces, and potentiates into a greater form that can be channeled into the shamanic task at hand—that of entering the sacred zone to petition the spirits for information, or to effect change. Change often has better chances of taking effect in those who, as cocreators, help to bring it about through their conscious participation. Drumming, dancing, and singing together to support a shared intention is a powerful way to create rhythmical empathy within a group.

The shaman in this particular vision began by opening to the spirits and asking, "Where is it that our circle needs to go tonight?" The spirits then led the way, mapping the journey to the tribe through the dance of the shaman. In some ways it was similar to the dance of the honeybee who pauses to map the location of the nearby pollen field to its hivemates.

For human beings, communal journeys into the sacred zone are journeys we can make together for our individual and collective well-being. (In fact one of the omissions of our culture, to our detriment, is that there is a lack of communal healing rituals.) Even when such a ritual is performed for the healing of a specific individual, the tribe itself is strengthened and brought to a greater level of cohesion and well-being. These beneficial results are magnified when the tribe itself participates directly in this healing process, in the gathering and sharing of spiritual pollen together.

At this point, the pinnacle of my healing and transformational work is in this area of rhythmical expression—dance— trance dance in particular. As a drummer and percussionist, I take immense pleasure in creating rhythms with an instrument, as well as having spirit play through me. Provided certain conditions exist, I find quick entry into the sacred zone through this pathway. However, for me, there is something different, more encompassing that happens when I put the drum or *shekere* down, step up and give my own body a wiggle and a shake. My body becomes the instrument, a direct link to spirit within and without, and responds back as these gateways to the numinous begin to open.

> To dance, then, is to pray, to meditate, to enter into communion
> with the larger dance, which is the universe.[1]

I call the type of dance I do ecstatic or trance dance. Essentially trance dance is a form of active meditation through authentic movement. It is a journey to the essential self. The rhythms and movements combine with the music to create an altered state of consciousness that allows entry into the sacred realm. Allowing the body, and parts of the body, to move to and express rhythms it finds engaging in the moment leads to this meditational state of mind and allows entry into a deeper mythic reality. In trance dance you encourage the inner wisdom of the body and your essential self to come forth and to flow with rhythms it finds appropriate and natural to itself. What is an appropriate rhythm? The rhythm the body naturally desires to move to, the movements it wants to make—not what our ego-selves project or deem appropriate.

Several years ago I was depressed and frustrated one night and had started gravitating to the dance as a form of self-directed therapy. I decided to put on one of my favorite CDs, *Initiation* by Gabrielle Roth and the Mirrors, and just dance. As I began to let myself go into the rhythms, my hands and arms began a motion as if pulling things from the environment into myself.

After a few minutes of this I came up to self-consciousness, observed my movements and said to myself, "Gee, isn't that being grabby. Since I am such a giving, got-it-together girl, that's quite enough of this now. Let me give my wealth of spirit back to the universe." What I failed to notice in that moment is that I was altering my dance according to the demands my ego was making in an effort to shore up its own self-image. Without realizing it, my ego was asserting its authoritarian voice across the homelands of the inner tribe.

So I altered my movements, not recognizing the faux pas I had just committed. The grabby motions were promptly put away and my ego now comforted itself by giving back to the universe in grand, glowing, gestures of abundance and sharing. But there was something wrong. These movements felt stilted and vapid. Although they may have been more aesthetic to view, they were contrived. Why was I feeling so lousy again?

Then it struck me. I was simply trying to mask the repulsion

I felt meeting the needy one inside. I was trying to turn my face away from her and pretend I didn't see. Aha! I paused in the dance, letting myself drift back to the needy one, calling to her, "Come back please and do your dance!"

Slowly she returned. As she became more present I was consumed by a torrent of impetuous motion. My arms flung out in the air before me, seizing the invisible food with tense fingers into clenched fists, stuffing it into my mouth, now a huge gaping hole in my contorted face, demanding to be filled. My arms moved more quickly than ever before in my life, and this time I didn't interrupt as they ripped through the air in front of me. A couple minutes later, the needy one was satiated, and I collapsed in a heap on my bed, panting furiously, a sheepish grin spreading over my face. Wow, did *that* feel good!

A review of ecstatic experiences reported by mystics and sages and ordinary folks reveals that ecstasy can sometimes arrive unbidden, out of nowhere it seems, as if slipping through a secret crack in the cosmic egg suddenly soaking you in its golden ambrosia. It can happen almost anywhere and anytime: while you're contemplating the beauty of a tree, dreaming a big dream, breathing, hiking, working in the garden, in a drumming circle, driving in a car. Abruptly and without warning, ecstasy can emerge out of the ethers and catch us in much the same way flypaper catches the fly—in mid-flight and unaware. No matter. If it seeks us out, or we woo it purposely to ourselves, it comes and sweeps us away in a most intense communion with something greater than the profane self we know so well.

Inviting ecstasy in a conscious way to join you as healer and teacher along your path is what the trance dance experience is about. It requires an intentional approach, like that the shaman uses to enter the mythic realm, as opposed to the unintentional, hit-or-miss flypaper approach. This is not to infer that the results of one are better than another, because they certainly are not. Ecstasy catching us unaware can be a much more powerful experience than when we invite it purposely to join us. I suppose because there is something utterly captivating, maybe romantically so, about being spiritually arrested in such an innocent and magnificent way. May we all be blessed with that kind of unanticipated grace now and then in our lives.

Before we cover some of the nuts and bolts of how to cultivate ecstasy through rhythm and dance, there's a bit more to sketch out contextually as we build a more solid framework to expand our exploration of what is to come.

Reaching ecstasy is a creative journey whose goal is something found in the totality of the journey itself. It's not a wonderful feeling that arrives at the end of completing a set of prescribed exercises or formulae. Ecstasy is a highly mercurial creature that enters you, suffusing your being in different forms and expressions. It carries its own agenda and timetable.

When you entrain to the rhythms of Soul an exchange of energy takes place, and within this exchange is knowledge and information. Knowledge you may not always be able to articulate verbally, but nonetheless, coherent in its own currency.

> Soul is not an abstract psychological or religious concept, but a way of feeling the rhythm of life itself . . . a rhythm that must be danced with.[2]

As I referred to ecstasy as a mercurial creature, I encourage you to think of it as a sentient being. One reason is that this recognition, this personification, plugs you into its deeper mythic tenure, and this is a natural form of perception to the shamanic archetype. Personifying ecstasy also fills life with Life, putting us in closer touch with soul. As Hillman comments,[3] "our imaginative recognition, the childlike act of imagining the world, animates the world and returns it to soul"; we are released from "that tight little shell of ego."

Personification is a form of empathy. Through empathy we form relationships to things we might otherwise perceive as inanimate and without Soul. Personification is the same impetus that informs the shaman's animistic way of being in the world. Personification urges us to the recognition of discrete beings and objects as "thous" rather than "its"—animals, rocks, objects, phenomena—the cosmos itself. Personification acknowledges the Soul in every thou. Ecstasy is experienced when we come into empathetic relationship with the inherent thous. Through personification, we, like the shaman, cultivate our relationships to all that is around us in both the physical and nonphysical worlds.

Ecstasy as a healing path, in the particular manner we're discussing, is all about coming into a deeper, more intimate relationship. You begin with your self, you and your own inner tribe, the inhabitants of the psyche. From here you extend this deeper relationship out to embrace the rest of creation, even if it's one thou at a time. Therein you find the doorway to the greater Soul.

I should mention here that while there have been many debates and theories about the nature and the existence of Soul, the model I work with here is Jungian-based, evolved further by James Hillman, Jean Houston, and others. I believe that Soul is synonymous with psyche and the essential self, and that it is inherently polytheistic, composed of a multiplicity of selves or sub-personalities. These emanations or projections are from deeper archetypal forces and mythic landscapes at the ground of Soul's being. The metaphor I give to this world of the Soul is the "inner community" or "inner tribe."

I can tell you one secret to a rich and healthy life with all certainty: it's *all* about relationship. As your relationships with your own inner world become more rich, honoring, and healthy, their essence reflect outwardly into the web of all your relations, enabling you to experience greater vitality and fulfillment in the larger stream of life.

When working with the idea "it's all about relationship," it's necessary to extend this perception into your inner community. If your relationships therein are estranged, and you deny, disrespect, or alienate some of your own inner beings, then the contents and quality of those relationships get played out as the external reality around you.

Since our culture does not yet put as high a premium on relationships and interdependence as it does on the gross national product and the bottom line, the importance of relationships tends to be transparent against the backdrop of the larger culture and socioeconomic imperatives that dominate modern life. It is usually in times of crisis that the importance of this extended web of relationship is brought to the fore of our minds, only to sink down, fade, or be replaced with cynicism when life returns to a semblance of "profane normalcy."

Because there is not much of an emphasis on the web of relationships in the outer world, except as fodder for a morals debate, the corresponding web of relationships in our inner world suffers as well. The depth at which you experience a healthy connection with the souls of others will be the quality and depth at which you experience a connection to your own. As within, so without.

I also believe that the resurgence of the goddess archetype and Earth-centered spiritualities is a collaborative response between anima mundi, the world Soul, and the individual souls of people drawn to this imperative. The goal is to help restore balance to the planet by addressing this lack of care and attention to the sphere of relationship that afflicts a large body of modern peoples, estranging them from soul and Soul.

Ecstasy is a great connoisseur of beauty, paradox, authenticity, and especially, community gatherings. If you are able to greet each member of your inner tribe along the way and invite them to join you in your journey, you are preparing a pleasing table for ecstasy. You can be quite certain that ecstasy will take notice, and chances are, it will gladly accept your invitation.

Ecstasy is about surrendering and letting go. While it is indeed a wonderful experience, the journey of ecstasy is essentially a series of "relational encounters" every step along the way. Inevitably, you will meet unfamiliar and sometimes difficult places and faces of your self through the dance: pride, fear, envy, insecurity, powerlessness, arrogance, and anxiety because ecstasy calls you to meet and relate to who you are in the moment, in the now. As you do, you come to share a closer mutual embrace with your essential self, your soul. All these beings you meet along the way are aspects of it, of you, faces of the multifaceted diamond that is your self.

The shaman understands that in order to more fully see, he or she must enter the darkness, the unknown, and meet the creatures and beings that dwell there—the fringe members of your inner tribe. For they are holders of knowledge and energy and have their role in the grand scheme. The challenge here is that they exist within various layers of the psyche, some more accessible to your queries, others hiding out within deep pockets of the unconscious, likely to spring forth into your profane affairs at the most inconvenient times. To contact them, sometimes it is best to loosen the reins on trying to do so and instead allow them to approach you. This is where trance dance can assist your efforts, for these inner tribal members will appear in the space of the dance from time to time. Also working with your dreams, and techniques such as active imagination, are extremely beneficial, for it is here that the creatures of the dark may express themselves more freely and openly.

Why is it even important to contact our fringe beings? This is where we revisit the importance of myth and the mythic imagination, for in terms of our healing needs, personally and collectively, it is from the realm of myth that all these inner beings are birthed within ourselves. We go to the mythic realm to engage and resolve the inner storylines and dramas that feed the fears and phobias that hold us hostage in varying states of distress in the profane world, just as the shaman journeys to the same realm to accomplish his healing work.

For this reason, it is highly advisable to have a goal, an intention to reach for through your flights of ecstasy. If you can stay loose and open on the contents and shape of the journey that takes you there, so much the better. A cultivation of courage, and especially willingness, to face the unknown are essential inner tools to take with you as you wade into the sentient flows of the deeper storied rhythms animating your life. For the psyche is always in motion, in its own inner dance of living change, a great river that pours into the ocean of Soul. We just lose touch with this great flow once in a while and fall out of its rhythm, as individuals and societies. We lose touch with the songlines singing through our soul. This is a form of spiritual malnourishment afflicting the lives of many today.

There is a story that popped up one night along a challenging bend of my ecstatic journey—*The Wizard of Oz*. I had met the judgmental person in myself and heard a voice respond, "Oh, you have no heart? Follow me!"

Then I met the frightened one. "You have no courage? Come, we're off to see the wizard!"

Another night I met the know-it-all. "You're an arrogant s.o.b.? Very well, want to join me on an adventure?" It may sound silly, but I've learned that these mythic story lines and characters present themselves to us for good reasons. It is beneficial to encourage them and animate them when they appear. They're also an effective antidote for the occasional overdose of taking yourself and life too seriously. So sometimes by the time you reach the wizard at the Emerald City of ecstasy, there may be a whole group traveling with you.

And you see that's the beauty of it. Ecstasy is truly a communal affair! It comes and gathers up all of who you are. It's all about being in community in its deepest sense. It is about being in relationship with yourself, creating ever-expanding circles of high synergy. It is the expression of connections and relationships to the thous in your inner community and the outer community at large. When the relationships you have to different parts of yourself are honest, authentic and honoring, they open up widening ecstatic pathways to an experience of wholeness and unity that transcend the feelings of isolation and separation that are typical of modern life.

Let's turn to some preparatory elements of dancing in the trance. The following can be done alone, or with a group of people.

Setting the Ambience: Creating the Container

A proper ambient setting is of utmost importance. By taking care here, you begin entering into a ritual state of mind, a feeling of respect and sanctity for what you are about to do. You seek to create an ambient atmosphere to support your transition into a meditative state of mind. It's not always an easy task to move away from the egocentric profane world. This is why taking care to set a conducive ambience is such an integral first step to your experience.

Lighting is a critical factor. It is probably one of the first things we notice about our environment. Setting ambient lighting helps us make the transition from mundane reality into sacred space more easily and completely. I recommend avoiding florescent fixtures at all costs. They are harsh and unnatural. Instead use candles, such as seven-day or others whose flames are safely enclosed. You can also use small tree lights strung about or colored light bulbs. In a larger setting, the use of spotlights with colored gels is very good as well.

Do include candles whenever possible, for it brings into your environment in a small but potent way, a semblance of the glowing light of campfires. Whether we realize it or not, this links us immediately back to our ancient shamanic roots, where people have drummed, danced, chanted, and entered communal trance and healing ecstasies around the sacred fire for millenia. I believe this ancient knowledge and experience is encoded within the well of collective human consciousness and deep within our flesh and blood.

When we set an atmosphere that resonates with some of these ancient and timeless elements, we begin to connect with these deeper memories, the deeper knowing, encoded within ourselves and our collective humanity. Call it a spiritual morphic resonance perhaps, per Rupert Sheldrake's theories, but whatever it is, it is there, and recreating elements of our ancient environments helps us tap into it, bringing the archetypal presence of the past into the now, directly shaping our contemporary trance experiences.

Deep down in our beings we all know the place inside where ecstasy lives. At most we've just forgotten, that is all. Healing through ecstasy is nothing new. It is probably the oldest healing method on Earth. So take care and enjoy setting your ambience. By doing so you are taking an important step in helping yourself remember who you are and what you already know.

As in many traditions, you may also wish to light some incense, sage, or sweet grass, and offer a simple blessing or prayer into the space you are creating. Invite your nonphysical friends, teachers, or guides to join you. Some may wish to call the elements and directions into the circle they are preparing. Others may reach toward the deity or deities of their faith. Whatever inspires you to feel the stirrings of the sacred, take this time to call their names.

Setting Intentions

At this point it is also good to take a few moments of silence to form an intention as a focus for your journey into the mythic realm. It might be as general as exploring you who are in the present moment through the dance. It might be to seek a new perspective on a challenging issue in your life. It may be to request healing for yourself, or for another. It may be to commune with the Earth or with teachers and guides that will be joining you. It may be to pump up an archetype in your life. You may wish to center on a quality you want to bring in, recover, or strengthen. You can also meet with a fear to discover the wisdom within or to release the energy it holds.

If you're unclear on an intention, consider using inner-work cards, such as the Native American *Medicine Cards, The Mayan Oracle,* tarot decks, and so on. Draw a card before you begin and use the image and its qualities as a way to focus your intention.

It is also advisable to dance just for the sheer pleasure of it now and then!

The Music

If you are using recorded music, I recommend a selection of songs that vary in tempo, beginning with slow. I also find that instrumentals and songs with a strong percussive line are conducive for trancing, more so than ballad-type vocals, although for some these may work. Give yourself appropriate music in the beginning, for the first ten minutes or longer, to warm up your body. Move to the music slowly, focusing on gently stretching and moving different parts of your body: head and neck, shoulders, arms, hands, hips, waist, knees, ankles, and feet. Suggestions for specific CDs for trance dancing are listed in the Resources section.

I also highly recommend Gabrielle Roth's video called "The Wave." It is a thirty-minute guided ecstatic experience of rhythm and motion, bringing you through a warm-up and allowing you to go deeper into trance dancing through the five sacred rhythms that Gabrielle has outlined in her book, *Maps to Ecstasy*: flowing, staccato, chaos, lyrical, and stillness. I won't explore this particular model in detail here, but if you feel an affinity for trance dancing, I encourage you to explore Gabrielle's work and her many CDs on your own. She has long been blazing trails into this ecstatic frontier, and in many ways has pioneered much of this work, which in turn has fed my own in profound ways.

Eyes: Closed, Open, Covered?

Here there is a greater variety to experiment with than perhaps first meets the eye (pun intended!). Closing or covering the eyes with a bandanna can assist in several ways. Keeping your eyes closed can help you withdraw from mundane reality and bring you deeper into your inner world. It can also facilitate a connection to the presence of teachers and guides in the spirit realm and to members of your own inner tribe. By closing your eyes, you can sometimes sense more clearly the deeper rhythmic patterns occurring within and around you.

I tend to spend a good deal of time dancing with eyes closed, experiencing the benefits mentioned above, although I have begun experimenting with a variety of alternatives with interesting results. The reason I began exploring this was due to observations I made while dancing within groups of people. While it was true that I had powerful experiences with eyes closed, it also tended to isolate me somewhat from the rest of the group. I could feel and hear them moving all around me, but I was very much focused and absorbed in my own dance. I'm not saying this isn't appropriate. There are many times when this is totally beneficial and healing, yet in the interest of exploration it should be said that there is another large world that lies beyond the trance of closed eyes.

Dancing in trance with eyes open allows you to experience other sublime aspects and options through your own dance and to connect more solidly with a dance partner or the circle of people you're dancing with. When you allow visual input to enter your trance, in essence you're expanding your inner world horizontally, to encompass the larger reality of the group's dance you are part of.

With eyes slightly open, you can observe how the rhythms of the various dancers blend together or diverge, and how they express the life and reality of a larger organism, the organism created by the circle of people as a whole. As I've worked with entraining to visual rhythms I've noticed that my feeling of connection to the larger group tends to increase and intensify this way. It's also been a great way to add dimension to the dance by opening up to the ways in which the visual rhythms around you can move and shape your own dance experience.

I have found that opening my eyes does lessen the strength of the trance state and the connection to my inner world, but I'm watching that change over time as I explore this more. There are a few techniques that are helpful in this regard. First, when opening the eyes in trance, open them softly, meaning very slightly or halfway open. Another technique that works well is to combine a slight crossing of the eyes while they are in this slightly open state. This increases visual-pattern acuity. Your eyes will perceive an overall flow of visual rhythms around you, which expresses itself in patterns of color and texture and movements instead of the discrete motions and objects we tend to see when we observe something straight on. Try it and you will see the difference between the two. A third technique is to veil the eyes with a semi-sheer material: just enough to alter visual perception, which is actually a timeless technique found in many cultures to help induce the trance state. Try including a crossing of the eyes here as well.

I've found that once entranced, if I can then gently blend visual impressions of the rhythmic movements of people around me, my experience and connection with the greater spirit moving with and through the collective group expand. I will usually go back and forth between open eyes and closed eyes. Something else that I often feel moved to do is to take a rattle or shekere or jingle sticks out on the dance floor. The women in the local drum and dance community often wear colorful flowing skirts that sweep around their ankles in arcs of color, which again enhance the trance experience in its own way. The key here is to feel open to experiment. What works for one person may not work as well for another. Search out what works for you.

Circular motions and spinning is also another way to induce an altered state of consciousness. If you begin to lose focus or feel you're going too far into an altered state, try touching the tip of your tongue to the roof of your mouth for a few moments. This

connects two major energy meridians of the body—the govern-
ing and central meridians. One ends at the tip of your tongue,
the other begins at the roof of your mouth. Together they complete an energetic circuit that circles your body front to back,
from the base of your spine to the top of your head. Touching
one to the other has a way of focusing energy and bringing more
clarity to your perceptions. Doing this is also effective if you begin feeling fuzzy from using cannabis to assist you in the trance
state. And while we're on that subject I will say that I find that
considered and sacramental use of psychoactive substances such
as cannabis is generally a complement to the trance experience. It
tends to increase perception of patterns on a kinesthetic and psychological level. I find that imbibing just enough to help "part
the veils" is as much as is needed.

Journeying on the Wings of Rhythm

So the ambience is set, along with your intention, and the music
is playing. With eyes closed, center yourself. Begin to follow the
breath in and out. Relax your jaw. It is amazing how much energy is held here. Whenever you desire to go deeper into the
rhythms, be sure that your jaw is relaxed. Invite the music into
your body. Drink the rhythms into yourself as deeply and gently
as you can, allowing them to guide you to your own inner rhythms.
Let your body begin to move or sway in whatever way it likes. If
it doesn't seem to have a particular desire, put it into motion
purposely, looking for what feels good to the body. You can be
light and playful. Turn on your sensual self. This is not somber
work. It is sacred play. You're seeking a connection, a communion with your inner world. You're courting and being courted by
your essential self, so let the wooing begin.

As you put your body into motion, follow what feels good in
a sensual way, and you will begin moving away from the ego's
chatter and preoccupation with ordinary reality. If you cannot
move away from this chatter within a few minutes, consider en-

ergizing it instead. Find a way to incorporate it into the dance and let it just move through you. Do not be surprised if you find your body entraining itself in an autistic kind of way to various rhythms. Just let your body go into a rhythm it finds entrancing for as long as it likes. Your dance is not about being technically aesthetic. It's about allowing your body and parts thereof to follow a rhythm it finds alluring and to let it move in the way it wants, for as long as it wants.

There is a paradoxical aspect to opening to ecstasy as I'm describing here, because, on one hand it involves purposeful intent, a goal to focus on. On the other, it requires a surrendering, a letting go. It is a give and take, your intention setting the tone of the work you wish to accomplish and the journey you wish to make, and then you surrender into the imagistic contents and rhythmical flow that ecstasy reveals to accomplish that work. How deep you go is directly connected to the willingness to let go and surrender into the experience. As Bradford Keeney aptly notes, "falling into this rhythm has less to do with know-how, understanding, or expertise. It has more to do with trust."[4]

Allow yourself to gently fall back into the arms of your inner community. Someone will be there to catch you. Open. Trust. Move. Nudge yourself. Let go into the flow.

As you open yourself and your inner senses, feel and imagine yourself as a rhythmic wave of energy blending with the music, a wave that moves within a larger eddy, your soul, which swirls in still larger rivers of life: your family, your community, the Earth, the cosmos. As you dance, know that the cosmos dances with you and through you. Bring this awareness to the fore of your mind. Let it light your curiosity. Let it arouse your imaginal mind.

At this point, I usually let go of holding my original intention in my conscious mind and put it off to the side. I will visit it now and again throughout the journey. As completely as possible, you want to immerse yourself in the rhythms of the music now, the rhythms of your body and of your surroundings—in a Zenlike way—with no thought, no mind, no judgments. Just feeling. Just being. Just being rhythm.

The intention at this point in the journey is to simply meet, engage, and dance with whatever archetypal forces, beings, teachers, or storylines that come to you, trusting that the dance and whatever comes through has everything to do with your original intention. Even if it doesn't seem to directly, then I suggest that the dance, if we are not trying to mold it into a certain form, reflects a dynamic connected to the original intention, something that needs to be met and integrated before moving on.

If you do not trust your moving body or do not feel at home in it, then this is a great place to start! There is an important guideline to cultivating ecstasy through dance: you must enter into *who you are in the moment.* Who you really are beneath the persona you show to the outside world. The dance allows you to connect with these places in yourself. The way to is through, not around. You cannot vault over challenges or bad moods to reach ecstasy. It's actually found by going within, embracing them, and moving through. The rhythms and dance of your body will guide you.

> Your body is the ground metaphor of your life, the expression of your existence. It is your Bible, your encyclopedia, your life story. Everything that happens to you is stored and reflected in your body. Your body knows; your body tells.[5]

One reason why ecstatic dance is so powerful on a psychological level is that all experiences get stored as memories in the body's tissues. Challenging experiences such as pain, trauma, or frustrations come to settle as snags somewhere in the ecology of the soul's forest. Ecstasy comes to nudge or shake this congested stuff out, letting it fall to the forest floor where it can enrich the soil of the soul. Through this process, the energy contained in these snags gets released and recycled into the greater system where the self can draw on it more freely again. It's important, therefore, to let the rhythms animate whatever parts of the body they want to go to, because most likely, that's where the emotional snags are stored in the physical tissues.

As you go through the dance, the trance will vary in levels of intensity. You will periodically cycle back up to self-consciousness. This is fine and a natural part of the process. It is useful as a place where you can revisit your original intention. It also provides the opportunity to look at whatever new material may be presenting itself to you in that moment through your ego awareness. The ego does indeed participate and play an important role in this process, for it too is a part of the self, and the soul seeks to collaborate with it in bringing healing and vital energy to the inner community. For example, when you return to self-consciousness you may feel vulnerable or find yourself showing off to an audience, either in reality, or in your mind's eye. Resist judging it, turning away, or being discouraged. Instead, scoop it up somehow, with a movement of your arms perhaps. Bring it into yourself and dance with it. Why not? There it is. Hang out with it in the rhythm. Keep moving. Let go into it. Let go into whatever comes up, moment to moment. Soon you will find yourself captivated by another rhythmic wave as it moves through you and takes you somewhere else. Encourage and support this collaboration, this communion between your ego and essential self, the efforts of the shamanic archetype as it performs the sacred work at hand.

People often report hearing voices, seeing images in their mind's eye, or having intense kinesthetic sensations during the dance, particularly when there is live drumming. "Advice" may come to you, especially if you put out such a request in the beginning. Carla, one of the members of the women's magical group, said that in our dance one night she was told to put her ear to the Earth and listen. She followed this guidance. She moved from dancing to put her ear to the floor for about ten minutes and just listened as we continued to dance around her.

She said that that simple act coupled with the healing rhythms of her dance moved something through her that she had been struggling with for days.

Morwen says she often feels shapes of energy moving with her. Sometimes she forms shapes with her mind as the energy comes to her. Other times shapes approach her as if coming from the ecstatic energy itself. I experience something similar. I often meet shapes and symbols that envelope and move through me: a triangle here, a spiral there, squares and circles and sometimes more complex geometrical patterns. I find my dance often traces the edges of these symbols with various parts of my body. It is beneficial to note these and bring forth the dance of shapes and symbols, for they can create a gestalt of the psyche. As music therapist Carolyn Kenny notes, "they convert energy into a different form, a form that can heal."[6] Symbols activate your inner resources.

Sometimes an animal will join you, particularly if you've been working with shamanism and totem allies. It's not unusual for such animals to come and merge with you and take you on a journey. Sometimes there is a great bird who visits me. It comes and invites me to fly alongside it. Other times we merge together as one, sharing the same wings and eyes as we fly through the mythic realm. Other spirit allies may come and dance with you. Entire story lines may emerge, which can be expressed through your dance, or just by visualizing them as you listen attentively to the music.

> Myths don't count if they're just hitting your rational faculties—they have to hit the heart. . . . And insofar as the myth is a revelation of dimensions of your own spiritual potential, you are activating those dimensions in yourself and experiencing them.[7]

If you are physically unable to dance, these experiences can still be available to you through more traditional forms of meditation and active imagination. My friend Kate, who was recovering from surgery and new to opening to ecstasy through rhythm and trance dance, reported the following the first time she tried exploring this through quiet meditation:

> I began my meditation as usual, expecting my mind to wander, but it didn't. A Native American chant began in my head, so I just went with it. Soon, a vision of a Native American dancer adorned with feathers and what looked like ritual dress popped into my head. I blended with the vision and felt myself dancing. Physically, I began to move my feet slightly to the rhythm of the chant. Suddenly a very distinct feeling of pressure began in the area of the first or second chakra and remained for some time. Then a tingling sensation began at the solar plexus that rose to the area of the heart chakra. I continued to chant and dance in my mind, when suddenly a strange sensation sort of buzzed in my brain. It was the strangest feeling I've ever had—but a terrific feeling! When it all subsided, I tried to reenter the chant-rhythm mode, but it was gone. It was a truly wonderful experience that lasted about forty minutes. Even the next day I could still feel a slight sensation in the area of my sixth chakra, like a remnant vibration that continued to ripple out long after the experience itself had ended.

In *A Mythic Life,* Jean Houston reports intriguing results of research she's performed over many years regarding the healing-creative power of visual imagery experienced through altered states of consciousness. She speaks of a cradle she and her husband Bob developed, based on the idea of the witch's broomstick. The broomstick was apparently a kind of cradle suspended from a tree "the movements of which affected the vestibular system so that the witch, who may also have augmented her journey with a dose of datura stramonium, felt that she was flying off to other realms." Their cradle allowed subjects to stand up in it and the subject's slightest movement would cause it to move from side to side, frontward and backward and in rotating circles. The subjects reported experiences similar to what Jean had encountered in her research of subjects on psychedelics. These experiences were highly imagistic and allowed the subjects to tap into vast reservoirs of creativity.

From studies of hundreds of subjects in the cradle, one of the things Jean and Bob concluded was that

> The inner imagery process appears to be essentially creative, tapping into domains of the self that are available all the time. . . . These other domains . . . offer vast reservoirs of unconscious knowledge and content to the creative process. The further into these domains one goes, the richer the solutions will be. . . . images observed long enough will cease to be random or disconnected and will organize into symbolic dramas, narratives, or problem-solving processes.[8]

Like the cradle, I suspect body motions experienced through authentic movement and dance can have similar effects on the inner ear and bring about an altered state of consciousness and this highly creative space Jean's subjects experienced. Spinning and twirling and dipping motions in the dance mimic the motions of the cradle. It is through this altered space of consciousness in the dance that the inner symbolic narratives emerge.

> . . . when mythic material remains latent, unused and unexplored, it can lead to pathological behavior. Release the latency, carry the story forward, and a miracle of liberation occurs in the psyche.[9]

By dancing with your visual, kinesthetic, or emotional images, by dancing the mythic storylines that emerge through ecstasy, you are dancing the mythic contents of your life. You are dancing with Life, engaging in it directly and purposefully. There is an incredible healing power contained in this simple act alone! You carry the story of your life forward. Dancing your life ritualizes it, makes it sacred. You are giving form to recondite realities that often tease the grasp of the rational. The dance allows you to experience directly the vigor and aliveness of these stories moving within you as well and provides a concrete form to witness and reflect upon them. Through the dance, you attend to the needs of the Soul to be known by you. The Soul in turn attends to your need to experience beauty and connections within the larger flow of life.

The dance shows you how to live in greater accord with the inner community. As you create synergistic relationships with your inner tribe, the effects ripple out far and wide into the greater circle of community. As another way to support your healing journey through the dance, it is helpful to record the contents of the dance upon finishing, either with words or pictorial images.

Explorations at the Edge

The spirit blows where it will, and lately it wills
to blow everywhere, carrying us into a spiritual
multiculturalism that seems to have its own agenda.
Jean Houston

Behold the circle
under the outstretched arms
of the Milky Way
The stars sing with the night birds
Beauty I am!
Joy! Joy!
Joy! Joy!
Joy!

The earth rises up, greets every footstep
gentle winds whisper
Beauty you are!
Joy! Joy!
Joy! Joy!
Joy!

Follow the song of your soul
a shimmering thread weaving itself
through the tapestry of life
Beauty we are!
Joy! Joy!
Joy! Joy!
Joy!

It is night and I am dancing beneath the stars. Twirling round the sacred fire, feet patting Mother Earth, arms outstretched to Father Sky move in great dipping motions. I'm aware of a great ladle hovering over my head filling me with manna overflowing into the sacred circle. The hypnotic pulse of the drummers and the sinuous movements of the dancers shape and excite the energy. It bathes the circle in a golden glow.

I move off to the side, out of the flow of dancers to catch my breath and behold the beauty of this organic communal ritual as it takes form around me. Nadu and Running Wolf are with me. Nadu whispers something into my ear.

I'd like to invite you to join me now on the cutting edge of exploring rhythmic empathy. We've touched upon the spiritual renaissance, the Great Awakening occurring across the planet; a new paradigm struggling to be born. This new paradigm is being circumscribed by "scientific" discoveries in the new physics and life sciences that confirm what shamans, mystics, and sages have been telling us for millennia:

○ We are one
○ Whatever we do affects the whole
○ Everything is alive
○ Consciousness creates reality

Many people feel this approach. A spiritual energy, a new vibration is how it is sometimes described. Matthew Fox refers to it as the "coming of the Cosmic Christ," and views this as an archetypal birth in the collective consciousness, which is referred to biblically as "the Second Coming."[10]

There is something coming, a way of living and being that is reaching for more wholeness and connection to the spirit, within and without. A body of knowledge, a mythic reality is approaching and its approach is being felt by increasing numbers of people, young and old, in all spheres of life in all cultures across the planet. The collective shamanic initiation crisis is meant to open the doors within ourselves that are currently closed or obstructed by egocentric hubris. Ecstasy is the philosopher's stone that, coupled with intent, allows the shamanic archetype, the Cosmic Christ within, to actualize the potential of this wisdom from its un-manifest form in the cosmos to concrete forms here on Earth, in everyday life.

From my own journeys into the mythic realm, my sense is that "new" is not the best word to describe the spiritual renaissance that is drawing near. What will be new is our application of it, but the approaching patterns themselves feel to be of a wisdom and body of knowledge that is very old. During this time we will be recognizing it, coming to know it again and integrating it with other pieces of knowledge we have gained from other paradigms. This integration will form a different picture of reality, one that appears to be more comprehensive and life-affirming than anything we have lived before in modern times.

As another way to say it, these approaching patterns contain the blueprints of a mythology of relationship that currently exist in a more latent, unrealized state. It is a mythology that is seeded with the perennial wisdom that exists deep within ourselves, and all spiritual traditions. It is a mythological pattern encoded within our DNA templates, now emerging within the firmaments of the psyche through the efforts of the shamanic archetype arising in prominence within the inner tribe.

We are poised at the edge of immense possibility. The times call us to be midwives to the birth of this great gestation.

Our increased ability for rhythmical empathy will provide crucial support to the shamanic archetype in birthing this wisdom into profane reality, anchoring it into the physical plane. Our task is to marry spirit and flesh, cross unknown thresholds and expand our explorations into this new territory.

The two primary streams of thought defining this task come from the communications given from Nadu and Running Wolf that night at the fire circle, coupled with the work of Jean Houston. There are many other works that also converge and support, but these are the two defining streams directing my inquiries and journeys in this area.

As I was standing at the edge of that fire circle, Nadu told me that music is being used to bring in the energy of this Great Awakening. Music has always been revered as providing human beings with a direct link to spirit and religious experience. Music always puts us in touch with our mythic reality, personally and collectively. Our knowledge and conscious awareness then that spirit is specifically using music to help infuse the qualities and contents of this new way of being within us, will increase our abilities to be conscious cocreators in the process. That is what's new—the growing awareness of this collaborative reality between the sacred and profane, between spirit embodied and spirit discarnate. There is a bridge between these worlds and we are building it together.

People across the planet are being inspired and will continue to be, to create new forms of spiritually based music that will carry the pregnant seeds of the Great Awakening further into our hearts and minds. This inspiration is being fed by a direct connection with spirit, in the form of guides, teachers, and allies, whether or not the recipients realize it. The inner work we do as individuals tills the dark rich soil of our soul to receive these seeds, which we in turn will tend and nourish in our own unique ways. We are apprenticed with spirit to be mapmakers of sacred fields wherein we may bring forth the blossom of the deeper dream we share in kind.

> Shamans transmit to their people in sign, song, and dance the nature of the cosmic geography that has been revealed to them in the process of initiation trances and soul journeys. Mapmakers and myth-dancers, shamans live internally in a multidimensional realm continuous with so-called ordinary reality.[11]

During this time we will witness the rise of a variety of spiritually based musical genres, particularly in the area of world music, and with it an increasing excitement for collaborations between musicians of various cultures. There is a swelling passion many feel for this multicultural musical dialogue, and it will continue to grow throughout the coming decade and beyond. Coupled with this, the urge to dance will also rise as people are moved by the pleasure of being embodied. Ecstatic dance is one way to develop hedonism to the high spiritual art form that is its greater calling. As we dance and make music together with an intent for healing, we visit the coming mythology and invigorate its potential.

> No, Jean, I think that if anyone can catch the content of this new myth, it will have to be those who are awakened to the imaginative life. It will have to be the artists and the poets, and certainly the dancers.[12]

Nadu also says it is important to preserve the traditional roots from which the music derives, for these roots give primal shape to the mythical roots of the spiritual heritage to come. As such, it is of utmost importance that these traditional forms be respected, honored, and preserved throughout time. This will allow us to more clearly sing in the myths of today from the roots of our past.

By the same token, the traditionalists need to support the evolution by encouraging the efforts of its progeny, and not seeing this departure as an act of betrayal or disrespect. These new forms of music are essential in providing a solid bridge for our mutual collaborations with spirit to manifest the greater potentials of this latent mythology. Musical dialogues across cultures, generations, and traditions are growing a solid container for the mythological patterns of this coming spiritual heritage to imbue itself in human culture.

At the level of physical human affairs, one attribute of this coming mythology is learning how to become more responsible in self-care and global citizenry. On a more esoteric level, this attribute is extended into a widened communion and collaboration with other forms of sentient beings, both physical and nonphysical. We will form partnerships of reciprocity with those in other realms for mutual care and well-being. How we can enter into this cocreative partnership with greater awareness through rhythm, ecstasy, and the dance is what we're about to explore, which we've been doing all along, but now, we step out a little farther.

Trance Dance as Divination

The deepest levels of consciousness can be discovered only through myth and ritual.

Carl Jung

To the universe belongs the dancer. He who does not dance does not know what happens.

Gospel of Thomas

In another study Houston conducted on fifty-five of the most creative thinkers, scientists, and artists in America, she found that most had taught themselves how to consciously delve into the rich reservoirs of depth realities and the imaginal realm. "They drew their insights not only from their own capacious minds, but also from the great creative archetypal realm wherein are 'stored' the principles that source new ideas and forms."[13]

In addition, she found that a majority of these people "felt they were partnered by an archetype." At times when they sensed this partnering, there was a feeling that they were two beings existing together, and that their local self was an exotype, or emanation of this archetypal presence. This type of partnering engendered an ability to perceive one's life and events from a wider, more universal perspective, and draw more directly on pools of energy and inspiration found within these deep worlds.

Jean herself feels partnered by an archetype, and in the last chapter of *A Mythic Life*,[14] she shares with us one of her many conversations with this being known as the goddess Athena. In that conversation, Athena assures us that she and all archetypes are indeed real, not simply lifeless constructs of the human mind. She also advises us to come into closer connection with the archetypal realm and the beings who reside there, for she says our mutual task is to collaborate in "the awakening." She says that in essence this closer relationship is similar to an exchange of nutrients between the worlds. "It becomes a healing exchange, with the archetype holding the higher 'pattern' of 'you' that can come through—not just for the healing of you but for the 'wholing' of you and the deepening of the world."[15]

Jean asks how we can come to know better the archetypal presence guiding our lives to strengthen our connection together. Athena summarizes by saying that "each must try to see his or her archetype in many ways—visually, kinesthetically, as felt or heard presence. *You must dance with us if you wish to know us.*"[16]

To know this archetypal realm better and the presence therein feeding us the higher blueprint of our life, we dance!

Over time, as I had been working with the dance, I observed that complex narratives and story lines were moving through me with increasing regularity. I also noticed that in these narratives a being or presence would join me in the dance and enact these story lines with me. It was an experience similar to being in touch with members of the Circle of Shaman, but these experiences were of a slightly different character. Whereas Nadu and Grandmother Illusion assumed roles primarily of a teaching nature, this other presence I met in the dance felt to be more a synthesis of companion, colleague, and older sibling.

Since I've carried this knowledge into the dance it has opened up to other levels of information. Kivana is my sister archetype in the mythic realm. She is the presence who comes to dance with me, the one who holds my higher blueprint. She tells me our relationship is one of reciprocity. What she offers me are her eyes, through which I may look out into the world with the ability to see from a greater universal perspective. What I offer her is the experience of a certain type of somatic wisdom found nowhere else but through the sensualities of corporeal form. She is able to extend herself into physicality through my flesh and mind, and I am able to extend myself into the greater patterns of existence through her sovereignty in the subtle realms. She holds the blueprints and through the dance I slip into them as I would another skin. The sense of heaven on Earth begins to emerge.

Jean also shared another word and concept that can be brought into the dance with your archetype: *entelechy*. Entelechy is a Greek word defined by Jean as "the dynamic purpose that drives us toward realizing our essential self, that gives us our higher destiny and the capacities and skills that our destiny needs for its unfolding."[17] Those in the archetypal realm are partnered with us in realizing this entelechy. It is possible that entelechy serves a dual purpose: to unfold our higher destiny and awaken us to the presence of our brethren and cocreators in the archetypal realm. These archetypal cocreators are enjoined with us in their destiny to minister the libation of our combined potential. We provide the spoon, they pour the elixir. We drink together.

> Indeed evidence exists that in certain states of consciousness, the mind-brain system appears to move into a larger wave resonance . . . when we meet myths and archetypes in this state, we can speak directly to the inner imaginal realm in which mind, nature, and spirit converge, and our highest potentials become available to us.[18]

With this in mind, there is another dance you can explore. As you enter the dance, call to your future self, the one who has journeyed through where you are today, navigating through these complex times and distilling the wisdom that you are reaching for. Within her lives your archetype and your self in close relationship. They make a highly creative partnership that is manifesting in form the dream you dream today . . . the dream of the Great Awakening. Invite her rhythms to move inside you, allowing that deeper exchange of knowledge and understanding between the two of you. Ask her to show you the dance you need to do to nurture the seeds of your becoming, to bear the fruit of your entelechy. Your future self will show you what you need to know, how you need to move through life to give birth to her and the dream in physical reality.

Another way to empower this experience is to make a mask of your future self or guiding archetype and to dance in a ritual space while wearing it. Create a costume to go with the mask. Shape-shift into that other identity as much as you can, and dance it.

The transformations you can experience on all levels of your being as a result of these mythic-realm journeys will be profound. Make note of how and when the results appear in your physical reality; the evidence of their effects will range from subtle shifts of feeling and attitude to more obvious external events and synchronicities. I've noticed that sometimes these changes happen rather quickly. Jean Houston has noted similar results and explains: "in an altered state of consciousness, especially when imagery is central to the experience, the mind enters into a different domain of time, and processes that should take weeks, months, or even years are done in hours, minutes, or seconds."[19]

These are dances I now do regularly, by myself, in partnership with others, and also in our women's magical group. These dances have become the focus for many rituals, with each of us realizing amazing results of a healing, wholing, and physically manifesting nature. For in a sacred circle when people entrain themselves to a common vision and intent when entering the mythic world, the ability to consciously shape reality is magnified exponentially. Through such experiences you divine the future into yourself, into the now. You divine the higher blueprint of Soul into your present life.

I joyously invite you to explore the sensations and effects in your life of opening to ecstasy through rhythm and the dance, alone and in larger circles to support your entelechy, your process of becoming, and the larger human collective. In reality it is a courtship dance, preparing yourself for a holy coupling with spirit to give birth to your self and the Great Awakening. So let the romance flow.

Epilogue

All shamans must join hands across the width of this green,
tumbling sphere you know as Earth; my pure life-giving Womb!
No matter how far the skies or wide the seas
you must join hands and start the Dance of Life!
Vusamazulu Credo Mutiva

Ecstasy is myth-shaping.
We are sprung from its seed.
We are shapers of the myth
Dancers of the dream.
Shapers being shapened
in the heart of ecstasy.
Kivana

In this modern age, the need for healing of the soul is great. No longer can the shaman exist in the mist of antiquity, no more can the shaman's role be limited to serving the small clan. As Grandmother Illusion foretold, the nature of shamanism on this planet is undergoing a transformation, so that rather than each shaman being an isolated point of light, all are joined together in a great weaving, cradling the Earth in a web of energy. Each of you reading this book is a part of the living web of light encircling the Earth as shown by Grandmother Illusion.

Every time we dance with ecstasy, the web among the worlds is energized and grows brighter, so that the Earth basks in the glow and the next bend along our healing journey is illuminated. Each time any of us recognizes another and weaves together the strands of our energy, the web grows stronger, to hold and guide the spirits of our communities and light the way for our children.

This is our responsibility and our joy: to travel ecstatic pathways into the sacred realm and back again, feeding the healing of ourselves, each other, and the planet with what we find there. May your imagination soar, may you fully enact the myth of your life, may the rhythms take you home to the ever-widening Circle of Shaman.

Notes

Chapter 3: Awkward Awakenings

1. Halifax, Joan (1982). *Shaman: The Wounded Healer.* New York: Thames and Hudson, p. 5.
2. Harner, Michael (1990). *The Way of the Shaman.* San Francisco, CA: HarperCollins, p. 20.
3. Eliade, Mircea (1964). *Shamanism.* Princeton, NJ: Princeton University Press.
4. Harner (1990).
5. Halifax (1982).
6. Eliade (1964).
7. Walsh, Roger (1990). *The Spirit of Shamanism.* Los Angeles: Tarcher, p. 142.
8. Halifax (1982).
9. Walsh (1990), p.142.
10. Feinstein, David, and Stanley Krippner (1990). *Personal Mythology: Using Ritual, Dreams, and Imagination to Discover Your Inner Self.* New York: Tarcher.
11. Larsen, Stephen (1976). *The Shaman's Doorway: Opening Imagination to the Power and Myth.* New York: Station Hill Press, p. 9.
12. Walsh (1990).
13. Harner, Michael (1992). "Way of the Shaman," Workshop, April 24–25.
14. Doore, Gary, Ed. (1988). *Shaman's Path: Healing, Personal Growth, and Empowerment.* Boston, MA: Shambhala.

Chapter 4: Dark Night of the Soul

1. Sams, Jamie, and David Carson (1988). *Medicine Cards.* Santa Fe, NM: Bear & Co.

2. Halifax, Joan (1982). *Shaman: The Wounded Healer*. New York: Thames and Hudson, p. 26.

3. Heinze, Ruth-Inge (1991). *Shamans of the Twentieth Century*. New York: Irvington, p. 192.

4. Walsh, Roger (1990). *The Spirit of Shamanism*. Los Angeles: Tarcher, p. 39.

5. Eliade, Mircea (1964). *Shamanism*. Princeton, NJ: Princeton University Press.

6. Larsen, Stephen (1976). *The Shaman's Doorway: Opening Imagination to the Power and Myth*. New York: Station Hill Press, p. 62.

7. Eliade (1964).

8. Larsen (1976), p. 62.

9. Halifax (1982).

10. Larsen (1976), p. 65.

Chapter 5: Spiritual Talismans

1. Grof, Stanley, and Christina Grof (1988). *The Stormy Search for the Self: A Guide to Personal Growth Through Transformational Crisis*. New York: Tarcher, p. 67.

2. Fox, Matthew (1988). *The Coming of the Cosmic Christ*. New York: Harper & Row.

3. Doore, Gary, Ed. (1988). *Shaman's Path: Healing, Personal Growth, and Empowerment*. Boston, MA: Shambhala, p. 23.

4. Eliade, Mircea (1964.) *Shamanism*. Princeton, NJ: Princeton University Press.

Chapter 6: The Power of Myth and the Mythic Imagination

1. Keen, Sam, and Anne Valley-Fox (1989). *Your Mythic Journey: Finding Meaning in Your Life Through Writing and Storytelling*. Los Angeles, CA: Tarcher, p. xi.

2. Keen and Valley-Fox (1989).

3. Walsh, Roger (1990). *The Spirit of Shamanism*. Los Angeles: Tarcher, p. 254.

4. Campbell, Joseph (1988). *An Open Life*. New York: Larson Publications, p. 5.

5. Houston, Jean (1996). *A Mythic Life: Learning to Live Our Greater Story*. San Francisco, CA: HarperCollins, p. 99.

6. Hillman, James (1989). *A Blue Fire*. San Francisco, CA: HarperCollins, p. 3.

7. Houston, Jean (1996). *A Mythic Life: Learning to Live Our Greater Story*. San Francisco, CA: HarperCollins, p. 97.

8. Feinstein, David, and Stanley Krippner (1988). *Personal Mythology.: Using Ritual, Dreams, and Imagination to Discover Your Inner Self*. New York: Tarcher, pp. 212–213.

9. Ferguson, Marilyn (1990). *Pragmagic*. New York: Pocket Books, p. 2.

10. Kenny, Carolyn Bereznak (1982). *The Mythic Artery: The Magic of Music Therapy*. Atascadero, CA: Ridgeview, pp. 36–37.

11. Walsh, Roger, and Francis Vaughn, Eds. (1993). *Paths Beyond Ego*. Los Angeles: Tarcher, p. 190.

12. Ibid., p. 191.

Chapter 7: The Shaman's Evolving Role in a World in Crisis

1. Feinstein, David, and Stanley Krippner (1988). *Personal Mythology.: Using Ritual, Dreams, and Imagination to Discover Your Inner Self*. New York: Tarcher, pp. 212–213.

2. Halifax, Joan (1982). *Shaman: The Wounded Healer*. New York: Thames and Hudson, p. 11.

3. Ibid.

4. Perkins, John (1994). *The World Is as You Dream It: Shamanic Teachings from the Amazon and Andes*. Rochester, VT: Destiny Books.

Chapter 8: Portals of Rhythm

1. Redfield, James (1993). *The Celestine Prophecy*. Hoover, AL: Satori Publishing.

Chapter 9: Elements of the Ecstatic Realm

1. McKenna, T. (1993). *Omni* magazine, May, p. 92.
2. Doore, Gary, Ed. (1988). *Shaman's Path: Healing, Personal Growth, and Empowerment.* Boston, MA: Shambhala, p. 29.
3. Redfield, James (1993). *The Celestine Prophecy.* Hoover, AL: Satori Publishing, p. 107.
4. Campbell, Joseph (1988). *An Open Life.* New York: Larson, p. 24.
5. Doore (1988), p. 29.
6. Neihardt, John (1979). *Black Elk Speaks.* Lincoln, NE: University of Nebraska Press, p. 43.
7. Doore (1988), p. 30.
8. Ibid., p. 24.
9. Metzner, Ralph (1986). In *Gateway of the Heart* (Sophia Adamson, Ed.). El Verano, CA: Green Earth Foundation, Foreword.

Chapter 10: Opening to Ecstasy

1. Flatischler, Reinhard (1992). *The Forgotten Power of Rhythm.* Mendocino, CA: Liferhythm, p. 16.
2. Keeney, Bradford (1996). *Everyday Soul.* New York: Riverhead Books, p. 84.
3. Ibid., p. 86.
4. Ibid.
5. Kenny, Carolyn Bereznak (1982). *The Mythic Artery: The Magic of Music Therapy.* Atascadero, CA: Ridgeview, p. 69.

Chapter 11: Trance Dance: Healing Through Ecstasy, Rhythm, and Myth

1. Houston, Jean (1996). *A Mythic Life: Learning to Live Our Greater Story.* San Francisco, CA: HarperCollins, p. 71.
2. Keeney, Bradford (1996). *Everyday Soul.* New York: Riverhead Books, p. 75.
3. Hillman, James (1989). *A Blue Fire.* San Francisco, CA: HarperCollins, p. 99.

4. Keeney (1996), p. 83.

5. Roth, Gabrielle (1989). *Maps to Ecstasy: Teachings of an Urban Shaman*. San Rafael, CA: New World Library, p. 29.

6. Kenny, Carolyn Bereznak (1982). *The Mythic Artery: The Magic of Music Therapy*. Atascadero, CA: Ridgeview, p. 39.

7. Campbell, Joseph (1988). *An Open Life*. New York: Larson, p. 35.

8. Houston (1996), p. 196.

9. Ibid., p 98.

10. Fox (1988).

11. Halifax, Joan (1982). *Shaman: The Wounded Healer*. New York: Thames and Hudson, p. 66.

12. Campbell (1988).

13. Houston, Jean (1996). *A Mythic Life: Learning to Live Our Greater Story*. San Francisco, CA: HarperCollins, p. 111.

14. Ibid., p. 82.

15. Ibid., p. 319.

16. Ibid.

17. Ibid., p. 125.

18. Ibid., p. 81.

19. Ibid., p. 197.

Resources

A Sampling of Trance Dance Music

DEAD CAN DANCE:
  Spirit Chaser
  Into the Labyrinth

BRENT LEWIS:
  Primitive Truth
  Jungle Moon

PROFESSOR TRANCE AND THE ENERGIZERS:
  Shaman's Breath

GABRIELLE ROTH AND THE MIRRORS:
  Any titles. Personal favorites: *Luna, Waves,* and *Initiation*

BABATUNDE OLATUNJI, MURUGA AND SIKIRU:
  Cosmic Rhythm Vibrations

TULKU:
  Trancendance

YULARA:
  All is One

HAMID BAROUDI:
  City No Mad

MICHAEL FITZSIMMONS:
  Light in the Village

NORTH SOUND:
  Nature's Drums

WORLD DANCE BEAT:
  Compilation

Web Sites of Interest

Earth Drum Council: http://www.earthdrum.com

> Organization cofounded in 1990 by Jimi and Morwen Two Feathers, empowering people through the drum and dance. Includes articles of interest, regional drum and dance events and workshops, and other links.

Waking World: http://www.waking.com

> An interactive site promoting positive global transformation. Discussion boards, including Trance Dance and Drumming, on-line seminars, selected products and gift items, and more.

Author's web site: http://www.tiac.net/users/newdream

> Writings on drumming, dancing, shamanism, and the ecstatic experience, personal anecdotes, and workshop information.

Comment and feedback are welcome and may be forwarded to the author electronically at Karen@earthdrum.com.

Index